A Wolf's Unlikely Mate

A Wolf's Unlikely Mate

Highland Shifters Book 1

Caroline S. Hilliard

Produced in Norway.

ISBN: 979-8-4209-5719-6

Copy edited by Lia Fairchild

Cover design by Munch + Nano
Thank you for creating such a beautiful cover for my story.

CONTENTS

ABOUT THIS BOOK

He's a werewolf. She's human. When a chance encounter leaves them both craving more, will his shifter secret scare her away from true love?

Jennie has been looking forward to her vacation in Scotland with her two best friends and their husbands. Life has been rough since her divorce, and this trip will give her a chance to refocus and take control of her life. If it wasn't for Michael's unwanted attentions, the single man her friends have invited on the trip to keep her company.

Sudden turbulence on the plane lands Jennie in the arms of a man. Big, strong, and gorgeous, Trevor is lust-worthy and more. When he later prevents a thief from getting away with her purse in the airport, Jennie is in captivated. But he disappears before she can get to know more about him. Knowing only his first name, she has no way to find him.

However, Jennie is in for a surprise when they arrive in Fearolc, their destination on the west coast of Scotland.

Trevor can't forget the blond beauty from the plane. Her smile, and the way she felt pressed up against him, has his protective instincts going into overdrive. Not to mention other basic instincts.

But if he knows what's good for him, he'll stay away from her. Jennie is human and getting involved with her can only lead to misery. As an alpha wolf he is expected to mate an alpha female. A human can only be a temporary distraction.

There is only one problem. She is going to be staying in Fearolc, at a cottage just a few hundred yards from his estate. And he might not be able to stop himself from seeking her out.

This work is intended for mature audiences. It contains explicit sexual situations and violence that some readers may find disturbing.

CHAPTER 1

Jennie couldn't believe she had let Ann and Marna talk her into going to Scotland with them. Standing in line for security at the airport, she regretted saying yes. There was nothing wrong with going to Scotland, per se. Actually, she had always wanted to go there. It seemed like a wild and fascinating place with a lot of history. But going on a couples' vacation when you were single sucked, especially when said couples had invited a single male friend along, obviously to keep her company so she wouldn't feel like the third wheel.

If only they had told her what they had planned and given her a choice in the matter. But, no, they had invited Michael without even telling her about it. Jennie had found out this morning when she arrived at the airport, and he was waiting for her by the check-in counters like he was her boyfriend or something. Which he most certainly was not.

Michael wasn't bad-looking. He was about six foot two with short black hair and light-brown eyes. Not overly muscular but lean and fit. His face was classically handsome with high cheekbones and a straight nose. His personality, though, was something else entirely. Michael had a tendency to assume everyone found him irresistible and liked hearing his own voice more than listening to others. Jennie usually avoided him whenever she saw him at parties, but this time she was stuck with him for two whole weeks.

Jennie just couldn't understand how Ann and Marna thought she would hit it off with Michael. Had they even talked to the guy? He was nothing like their husbands at all. James and Carlos were both kind and generous men.

"You should've come with me to the priority line. My gold card allows me to bring a friend or family. We would've been in the lounge having a glass of whiskey by now." Michael's voice was loud, like he wanted everyone around them to know he was rich and superior. Rich, he was. Superior, not so much. Jennie cringed and wanted to pretend she didn't know him, but standing so close in the security line that wasn't an option.

"I told you I don't mind waiting. I've got an economy ticket, so this is where I belong. Why don't you go to the priority line, and I'll see you at the gate later? I've got some shopping to do, anyway."

"I'll wait, then we'll go to the lounge. There'll be plenty of time for shopping in Edinburgh."

Jennie sighed and kept her mouth shut. She was going shopping at the airport no matter what Michael had to say about it. She needed a new bikini, and she wanted to have a look around the shops. Besides, the urge to get away and do her own thing was even stronger with Michael clinging to her like a leech.

Ten minutes later they had passed security, and without saying anything to Michael, she grabbed her small backpack and purse and headed toward the shops. Hopefully, he'd get the message.

No such luck.

"Hey, the lounge is this way." Michael came up on her right and put his arm around her waist, steering her in the opposite direction of the shops.

Jennie felt her temper flare. This guy was just too much. She spun out of his hold and glared at him.

"I told you I'm going shopping. You can go to the lounge if you want. I'll meet you at the gate later." She spoke with a calm but firm tone. Starting the vacation by shouting at him would probably ruin it for everyone, and Jennie didn't want to do that.

"Okay, suit yourself." Michael shrugged and almost looked a bit hurt when he turned his back on her and walked away. Jennie immediately felt bad. Maybe she had been a bit too hard on him, but he wasn't her boyfriend, and he had no right to make decisions for her. This was her vacation and she had paid a lot of money for it. She was going to make sure she enjoyed herself, Michael or no Michael.

***

Michael was a bit taken aback at Jennie's reaction. He had expected her to play a bit hard to get. Women like her always did. But her outright hostile behavior wasn't something he had been prepared for.

Jennie was beautiful, and he had spoken to her a few times before. They had never hit it off for some reason, even though he had done his best to impress her. She always found an excuse to escape whenever he tried to strike up a conversation. But he had thought that wouldn't be an issue on this trip. According to Carlos, Marna's husband, Jennie had a thing for him, so when Michael was asked if he wanted to join them on their trip to Scotland, he had said *yes* instantly.

He sighed and walked into the lounge. A glass of whiskey was just what he needed. Then, he had to rethink how to approach Jennie. She obviously needed him to be even more direct in his effort to pursue her. Some women expected that. They wanted the man to demonstrate that he took charge and decided what was going to happen. He just had to make sure she understood he wasn't so into her that he would let her walk all over him. Jennie was beautiful but not the only woman in the world.

∞∞∞

They settled into their seats for the seven-hour flight from New York to Edinburgh. Jennie had never been to Europe before, and it felt like she was going on the adventure of a lifetime. For some people a vacation like this was nothing out of the ordinary, but for her it was huge. The only negative was Michael, but for the next few hours, he wouldn't be able to bother her. The girls had decided to sit together on the plane, and the guys were sitting a few rows behind them.

They would land in Edinburgh at about five in the afternoon local time and would stay in a hotel until the next morning. Then, they would travel by train to a small place called Fearolc on the west coast of Scotland. The cottage they had rented there for a week was close to the sea, and the area was supposed to be perfect for hiking and kayaking. There was also a whiskey distillery nearby that they planned to visit.

The following week they would spend in and around Edinburgh, seeing the sights and doing some shopping. It would be interesting to visit a city with so much history stored in its buildings. There was a chapel built all the way back in 1130 A.D. She had never visited a structure that old before, and she wondered how it would feel.

"Oh, I'm so happy you decided to come with us, Jennie." Ann smiled at her. "It wouldn't have been the same without you, you know. It has always been the three of us experiencing new things together."

Jennie smiled. Ann was right. They had stuck together since high school, experiencing a lot of firsts together and supporting each other through their late teens and into adulthood. "I've always wanted to visit Scotland. It will be nice to do it together."

"You didn't bring your laptop, did you?" Marna's amusement was obvious.

Jennie laughed. "Of course, I did. You know I need to write in order to expend my creative energy that will result from all the new impressions. I'd go crazy and drive you all insane otherwise."

"So, what's it going to be this time? Some sexy story involving a highlander?" Ann looked at her expectantly.

"Perhaps. I don't know yet. I know it'll probably sound odd to you, but I don't consciously decide what to write. An idea pops into my head, and I run with it to see where it ends up. It's more the story leading me than I leading the story."

"Don't you plan out the story at all before you write?" Marna's eyes widened in astonishment. "That's what we were taught to do in school. I hated it. It was always the most boring part of writing an essay. If I hadn't been required to write the outline first, writing essays and stories wouldn't have been so bad."

"I know. Writing school essays isn't the same as being an author. Now I can write whatever and however I please. It's totally different. Letting the story take its own course works for me, but I know authors who plan the whole story in detail before they start writing. We obviously have different preferences. But whatever works, right?"

It was nice just spending time with her friends again without any restrictions on time. No lunchtime ending soon, no calling it an early night because of work the next day. Hopefully, this vacation would afford them some time to catch up on each other's lives.

Jennie had mostly kept to herself the last couple of years, not spending as much time with her friends as she used to. Ever since her painful divorce, it had been difficult for her to be around them. Every time she saw them, she was reminded of their marital bliss and her own failure to achieve the same.

But when Ann and Marna had asked her to come with them to Scotland, Jennie had come to a decision. The hurt and anger that controlled her life had to go. She couldn't let the failure of her marriage destroy the rest of her life. It was time to put her old life away and start a new one, and a trip to Scotland would serve as the kick-off for her fun and adventurous new life.

The breakfast they were served wasn't fantastic, but it was better than she had expected. They were flying coach, much to Michael's horror. He had probably never done that before, coming from a rich family. Jennie, on the other hand, had no idea what it was like to fly anything other than coach. Hell, she hadn't even been on a plane more than a couple of times before.

"I need to find the restroom." Jennie was sitting by the window, which was her favorite seat, but it meant that everyone between her and the aisle had to move every time she needed to get out for some reason. Ann and Marna got up and moved into the aisle, allowing Jennie to get out of her seat.

"I'll stretch my legs a bit while I'm up. Do you want me to get you something?"

Ann and Marna both shook their heads. Ann got an amused look in her eyes. "Don't go far, though. You might get lost."

Marna chuckled. "Yeah, and then we'd have to go looking for you. Or, maybe we'd get the flight attendant to issue an alert for everyone to keep an eye out for you."

Jennie laughed. "I think I'd find a hiding place and stay there until we landed if you did that."

She walked down the aisle and found the restroom. It was a small claustrophobic room, but it didn't bother her. After washing her hands, she exited and walked down the aisle to the middle section where she could cross over to the aisle on the other side. Just as Jennie rounded the corner to pass the stairs going up to the second story of the aircraft, the plane lurched, and she pitched forward toward the other side of the plane.

Strong arms caught her around her middle, and before she knew what was happening, she was trapped with her back against the wall next to the staircase. Her front was pressed up against a tall hard body. The plane was shaking and lurching, and she threw her arms around the man's body and fisted her hands in his shirt to hold on.

There was a ding and an alert over the speakers telling everyone to find their seats and put on their seat belts, but Jennie had no intension of moving at that moment. Not that she would have been able to if she tried. The man was keeping her tightly squeezed between the wall and his body. He was like a full body safety harness, a sturdy one, keeping her firmly in place. She felt safe. For some reason, she just knew this guy would never let anything happen to her. He would keep her safe if at all possible. Call it instinct, but Jennie had total confidence in him, a stranger.

The shaking eased, and she looked up into a pair of warm brown eyes framed by thick black lashes. He was tall, probably about six foot four, and his face was ruggedly handsome. He looked like a man who spent a lot of time outside, sporting a deep tan and a very becoming five o'clock shadow. His sandy-blond hair was short and a bit messy.

"Thank you. I think I'd have hurt myself it you hadn't been there to save me."

"My pleasure, ma'am. Are you all right?"

She nodded. "Yes, I'm perfectly fine, thanks to you."

He smiled and she almost gaped at him. The guy was gorgeous.

He released his hold on her, and Jennie realized she was still holding onto him with a death grip. She let go of him, and he took a step back.

"I'd better get back to my friends. They're probably worried about me." She smiled at him before turning away and walking back to her seat. Her heart was hammering in her chest, and she felt a bit breathless. But it had nothing to do with the turbulence.

Ann and Marna were both relieved to see her.

"Thank goodness, there you are." Marna's voice was a bit shaky. "Are you hurt?"

Shaking her head, Jennie smiled. "No, I'm fine."

Her friends got out of their seats to let her pass.

"How are you holding up, Marna? I know you're not a huge fan of flying." Jennie studied her friend's pale face. For some reason Jennie had never developed a fear of flying even though her own parents had died in a plane crash years ago.

Marna took a deep breath. "I'm hanging in there. Turbulence is common, right?"

"Yes, I've experienced it lots of times." Ann's voice was confident. She was traveling a few times a year as part of her job and was the one among them most accustomed to flying.

ooooo

Trevor could still feel the woman's breasts pressed up against him. Soft and squeezable, definitely real. If he hadn't held on so hard to keep her from falling and hurting herself, his hands would have been itching to touch her breasts. Which was all kinds of wrong, considering she was a stranger and in need of his help.

She had looked into his eyes, and he hadn't wanted to let her go. She was beautiful with pale porcelain skin and dark-blue eyes. Her long blond hair was pulled back into a ponytail showing off her graceful neck. And when she smiled, pulling his attention to her soft pink lips, all he could think about was tasting her mouth.

Then she walked away, and he had been left standing there, debating whether to go after her or forget about her. The flight attendant telling him to find his seat had snapped him out of his discussion with himself, and he had gone back to his first-class seat upstairs.

He settled back into his large seat and closed his eyes. The seat was comfortable enough, but his pants were a bit tight in the groin area. Trevor sighed. It was still a few hours until they were going to land, so he might as well try to get some sleep.

CHAPTER 2

As usual Jennie had packed too many clothes. Her suitcase was filled to capacity and then some, mostly because she wanted to be prepared for all kinds of weather. To her knowledge, you could end up getting temperatures ranging from thirty to ninety degrees in the summer in Scotland, and rain, hail, and strong winds weren't unusual. So, she had made sure she was prepared for everything.

The others had gone ahead through customs already. Jennie had assured them she would be fine on her own and had dismissed their attempt to stay behind with her, insisting it would be best if they went ahead and found out how to get to their hotel. As expected, her oversize bag was the last one to appear on the baggage belt.

Jennie was pulling her heavy suitcase off the baggage carousel when she felt a tug at her shoulder and turned around to see a man zigzagging through all the other passengers with her purse in his hand.

"Hey, get back here," she yelled and pointed. "Somebody stop him. He's got my purse."

Jennie could only watch as the man ran away from her with her wallet, phone, and passport. She quickly realized there was no way she was going to be able to catch him even if she tried. He was too fast.

She sighed in defeat. This would seriously affect her plans to have a good time. With no means to pay for anything, enjoying her stay there would all depend on being able to borrow money from her friends. And if that wasn't bad enough, she would have to contact the American embassy about her stolen passport.

As she watched the man's back weaving through the people in the big baggage hall, he suddenly flew to the right like he had been hit by a train or something. Jennie was unable to see exactly what was going on, but a few seconds later, she noticed a tall, muscular man walking toward her. The guy from the plane was looking directly at her, and when he got a little closer, she saw he was carrying her purse.

The relief she felt was so immense she felt her lips widen in a big grin. The big bear of a man had just saved her again and prevented her vacation from being ruined.

His face broke into a big smile as he approached her. "I believe this is yours, ma'am."

Jennie nodded, and without even thinking about it, she threw her arms around his neck and gave him a big hug. "Thank you. You must be my guardian angel or something."

"Or something." His voice was a dark rumble next to her ear.

The man's hands came up to hold her sides just

above her waist, and they felt so big and warm through her thin shirt. Her nipples tightened in response to the feel of his hands on her body, and she felt herself blushing furiously. It had been a long time since she responded like this to a man, and to a stranger no less. Mind you this was the second time she was squeezed up tightly against him in just a few hours, quite intimately for someone she had just met.

Jennie unhooked her arms from around his neck and pulled back. His hands slid to her waist, and then he let go of her as she took a step back from him. Her face was still flushed, but that couldn't be helped.

She met his warm brown eyes. He was smiling down at her, and she opened her mouth to say something, but nothing came out.

"I'm Trevor." His deep rumbling voice seemed to send a vibration through her body, and she felt her nipples tighten even more to form sharp points against the inside of her bra.

"Jennie. And again, thank you." She found her voice, and the words rushed out. "Now I don't have to put my vacation on hold to get a new passport, and figure out how to get money transferred from my account without any form of ID. I should've run after him, but then I'd have to leave my suitcase—"

"No, you should never take on a thief like that by yourself. He'd hurt you." Trevor was serious when he stared into her eyes. "It's not worth it. Your safety is more important than a passport and money."

Jennie nodded, too stunned to say anything. It almost sounded like a command and could be taken as a chauvinistic remark, but it wasn't. Deep down she knew he'd said it because he was genuinely concerned and didn't want her to get hurt, not because he didn't want her to stand up for herself.

"Let me carry that for you." He grabbed her large suitcase and lifted it like it weighed nothing. "Are you staying here long?"

A bit stunned, she fell into step beside him as they headed toward customs. "Um, two weeks."

"A big suitcase for two weeks. You come prepared for everything, don't you?" The amusement in his eyes when he looked at her had her blushing all over again.

"I read that the weather can change a lot around here, and I plan to spend a lot of time outside."

"Not just in Edinburgh, I hope?"

"No, we're going to stay in a small place called Fearolc for a week."

For a second there was astonishment in his eyes, before his expression became neutral.

Jennie studied his face. "Have you been there?"

Trevor nodded but didn't meet her eyes. "Yes, it's a nice place. Just don't walk around outside after dark. The terrain is uneven with a lot of rocks and cliffs. It's easy to hurt yourself when you can't see where you're going."

"Okay, thank you for the advice." Jennie got a strange feeling there was more behind his warning than just rough terrain, but she decided against asking him. She didn't want him to feel that she suspected him of keeping her in the dark about something.

They passed through customs, and Jennie saw her friends standing outside a coffee shop. "My friends are waiting for me over there." She pointed.

Trevor didn't say anything as they approached her friends, and he stopped a few yards short of reaching them.

She turned to him as he put her suitcase down. "Thank you, Trevor. I would've been really miserable right now if it wasn't for you."

"My pleasure." A warm, genuine smile spread across his face, and he suddenly reached out and grabbed her hand. Keeping his eyes locked on hers, he brought her hand up and brushed his lips over her knuckles in a brief kiss. Then, he let go of her hand and gave her a small nod before walking away.

Jennie stood there in shocked silence, watching his broad, muscular back as he moved away through the crowds of people in the busy airport. There was a feeling of loss in her chest, and she wanted to run after him.

"Who was that?" Ann's voice startled her, and she turned around to see everyone's eyes were trained on her. Ann and Marna looked amused, James and Carlos appeared to be confused, while Michael looked angry, whatever that was about.

"That was the man who just prevented my vacation from going down the drain." Jennie turned to see if she could still catch a glimpse of Trevor in the crowd, but he was gone. "A guy stole my purse and was getting away when Trevor knocked into him and got it back for me. No money, passport, or phone would've seriously dampened my vacation enthusiasm. I should've offered him something in return for his help."

ooooo

Walking away from Jennie shouldn't have been that

difficult. He had just met her a few hours ago. But as Trevor made his way through the airport toward the exit, all he could think about was her amazing scent of chocolate and strawberries and the feel of her soft breasts against his chest.

Trevor had been taken by her as soon as he saw her. She was beautiful…and that smile. It was like watching the sun going down into the sea with the warmth shining in her dark-blue eyes.

He had been watching her from a distance in the baggage hall, unable to take his eyes off her. The guy stealing her purse had been like a gift from the heavens, providing Trevor with the opportunity to come to her rescue, again. And it had been worth it. That amazing smile, and then she had launched herself around his neck, letting him feel her amazing body against his again. He had to force himself to let her go when she stepped away from him.

"Damn," Trevor swore aloud. He should have asked for her phone number or at least given her his, but he hadn't really been able to concentrate in her presence. She took his breath away. It was a wonder he had been able to speak at all. And then chastising her for the weight of her suitcase. He had acted like a moron or a teenager, unable to behave like a normal person around a beautiful woman.

Shaking his head at his own behavior, he strode outside to the big black four-by-four waiting for him by the curb. He put his small bag in the back before moving to the passenger side door.

"Good afternoon, sir. Nice to see you again." Duncan grinned from the driver's seat when Trevor opened the door and got in.

Trevor felt his lips stretch into a smile at Duncan's joke. "Nice to see you again, too, Duncan, but stop calling me sir. It makes me feel old, and I'm not that much older than you."

"Sure." Duncan's amusement was evident in his voice.

They pulled away from the curb and headed toward the M9. It would take about four hours to reach his house on the west coast.

At least there was a chance he would cross paths with Jennie again. He had been shocked when she said they would be staying in Fearolc for a week. His house was on the outskirts of the small village, and it was a peaceful place. There wasn't typically a lot of tourists since there was no overnight lodging in the area, and the lack of accommodation was not by accident. Most of the people living in the area weren't human, as the name Fearolc would suggest. Fearolc in Gaelic meant werewolf, and the few humans staying in the area were either mated to a werewolf or descendants of families that had been living in the area for a long time. Having a lot of tourists staying in the village could lead to unfortunate incidents.

"Who's renting out their cottage to tourists in the area? Do you know?" Trevor studied Duncan's face to gauge his reaction.

Duncan's expression darkened. "Yes, it's the Millers. We tried dissuading them, but they had already signed contracts with tourists for two weeks. The first group of six Americans will arrive tomorrow and stay for a week, and next week a family of four from Norway will be staying there. People know not to shift during the day at this time of the year, but we'll have to be extra careful at night as well for the next couple of weeks. You never know when some of these foreigners venture out at night. There will be a lot of trouble if they see a large wolf running around."

"Fuck! The Millers know better than to draw tourists into the area. What are they trying to do, out us?" Trevor was more than a little annoyed, but at least there was a positive result from this. He would see Jennie again. He would make sure of it.

ooooo

Michael was furious. They were on the tram going into the city center, and he was sitting in a seat by himself, cursing his own stupidity. Jennie had been adamant that she would get her own suitcase, and he didn't want to press the issue. It was a fine balance between taking charge and making it seem like he really cared about her, and the last part wasn't how he wanted to play this. But apparently, he should have stayed with her. The looks she had given the big beefcake made him want to scream in rage. All admiring and gooey-eyed, and the guy had played into it by kissing the back of her hand.

Well, at least she wasn't going to see that guy again. He was gone, and as far as Michael could tell, Jennie hadn't arranged to meet the beefcake again. It was time for Michael to show her what she needed and wanted in a real man.

ooooo

Jennie used her key card to get into her hotel room.

Putting down her heavy old-fashioned suitcase, she had a look around the small room and the adjoining bathroom. She breathed a sigh of relief and contentment. The rooms were clean and appeared to be newly refurbished.

Michael had insisted on carrying her suitcase to her room, and she had let him. But as soon as they had reached her door, she had excused herself and escaped into her room before he could make any attempt to follow her inside. Perhaps she was imagining things, but she got a feeling that was what he was planning to do, and Jennie wanted to avoid having to tell him no.

It was half an hour until she was going to meet the others in the lobby to go find a restaurant, and she wanted to take a shower. Jennie opened her suitcase and found some new clothes. There was no point unpacking since they were leaving first thing in the morning.

After a nice refreshing shower, she dressed in a dark-blue, knee-length skirt and a pale-pink top. She put on her shoes and a light jacket and grabbed her purse on her way out of the room.

The others were already in the lobby, ready to go, and they decided to walk to the restaurant. It was only a ten-minute walk from the hotel, and it was still sunny outside. This far north the sun set much later than she was used to in the summer.

They walked along the sidewalk and weaved their way through locals and other tourists. Jennie ended up walking beside Michael since the other couples walked together, but she was so busy taking in all the new sights that she didn't pay him much attention, and fortunately, he didn't try to initiate a conversation with her either.

The feel of this city was so different from any other city she had been to before, and all her senses were on overdrive, absorbing everything. The castle on the hill was magnificent, and she was looking forward to going back to the city in a week and having a closer look at it. But even walking through the streets, there were plenty of old buildings to take in, and the fact that the city was built on several ridges made it even more interesting.

Sensory overload was probably the reason she didn't notice the little girl with an ice-cream in her hand until she felt something brush against her leg. Jennie looked down to see ice-cream smeared across her skirt and groaned. Well, it probably served her right for not watching where she was going.

"Why don't you watch your kid? She's getting ice-cream on everyone. It's fucking disgusting."

Jennie's head snapped up in shock at Michael's angry outburst. "Michael, calm down! It wasn't her fault. I should've kept an eye on where I was going." She turned toward the child's mother, who was scowling at Michael. "I'm so sorry. He doesn't have any manners."

The woman smiled at Jennie before looking at her skirt with an apologetic expression on her face. "I'm sorry about your skirt."

Jennie smiled back. "It's okay. I'll wash it. What are washing machines for, right?"

Michael's grunt drew Jennie's attention to him. She glared at him before turning and walking briskly after the others. They were just opening the door to the restaurant when she caught up with them.

Ann looked at her skirt with raised eyebrows, and Jennie quickly explained. "A child with an ice-cream."

Ann laughed. "Yeah, aren't children amazing." The humor in her eyes soon faded to a longing look.

Jennie knew they were trying for a baby, but so far nothing had happened. They had only been trying for a few months, though, so it would probably happen soon.

"We'll find our table first, then I'll find a restroom and try to clean some of this off."

They were shown to their table, and she ended up between Michael and Carlos, Marna's husband.

Jennie quickly excused herself. "I'll be back in a little while."

CHAPTER 3

The server came up to the table, smiling, while Jennie was still in the bathroom. It was the perfect opportunity for Michael to make it up to Jennie by showing her that he would make sure she was always provided for. She would feel lucky to have a man by her side who knew what she wanted without her even having to ask for it.

Michael had fucked up by yelling at the mother of the small brat that had smeared her ice-cream all over Jennie's skirt. The mother deserved to hear the truth, but Jennie was too softhearted to realize that. Next time he wouldn't say anything in front of her. He should have known that swearing in front of a child would make Jennie mad. She was probably dying to have kids like every other unmated woman her age. That wasn't a feeling he could identify with at all, but he would have to give her a child at some stage. Not too soon, though. Children would take her focus away from him and what he wanted.

***

It took a few minutes to clean off her skirt. The ice-cream had soaked into the fabric, and Jennie had to use a lot of water to try to rinse it out. Thank goodness, her skirt was a dark color. At least it only showed as a wet patch and not a stain. She dried it as best she could with paper towels before going back into the restaurant.

As Jennie approached the table, their server was just leaving.

"It's okay. I ordered for you." Michael gave her a brilliant smile. He was good-looking, and a lot of women would be happy to have his smile directed at them, but Jennie got a picture of a smug cat in her head when she looked at him.

"What did you order?" She tried to make her voice pleasant, but she didn't quite manage to hide her apprehension.

"A chicken salad. We ordered a couple of bottles of red wine for the table too."

"Okay." Jennie turned around and hurried to the bar to get ahold of their server. Thankfully, they hadn't started preparing her food yet, so she was able to change her order.

On her way back to the table, she took a few deep breaths to calm her anger, and she was able to breathe a little easier by the time she sat down. While silently repeating to herself not to shout at Michael, Jennie turned to him with what she hoped was a polite smile on her face.

"Next time, please let me order my own food. You don't know me well enough to know my preferences, so please let me make my own choices."

"It's only right that a man orders for his woman." Michael looked a bit affronted.

Jennie couldn't help the snort she let out. "I'm not your woman, and I make my own choices, thank you very much." She glanced over at her friends, but each of the couples were talking amongst themselves and hadn't heard her and Michael's exchange.

Jennie purposefully turned away from Michael and stared at the bar. Thankfully, their server was on his way over with their drinks, and receiving their refreshments broke everyone out of their previous conversations.

The rest of the evening went by without any more disagreements with Michael. Her steak was tender and juicy, and it went well with the red wine her friends had ordered.

Back in her hotel room, she removed her laptop from her backpack. Jennie had an idea for a new paranormal erotic romance novel she would like to get started on. It was only ten o'clock at night, but with their flight leaving at five in the morning and the time difference, it had been a long day. But for some reason, she still wasn't tired.

The words poured out, and when she looked at the time after what felt like half an hour, she was surprised to see that it was already past midnight. After saving her work, she closed her laptop and put it back in her small backpack.

She went to the bathroom and brushed her teeth before crawling into bed but lying there, she found it difficult to relax. The story she had started on was occupying her brain, not allowing her to rest. It was like it wanted to be written down right then, its urgency pulling at her to finish what she had started. She had never felt anything like it before.

Jennie sat up with a jolt. She suddenly recognized the image in her head of the main male character in her new story. It was Trevor. She hadn't realized she had used him as a model for her story until that moment. How did she not see it before? Trevor was the perfect male character for her novel, and thinking about it, it was perfectly natural for her to build a story based on her unusual encounters with such an extraordinary man.

Lying back down, she recalled his beautiful brown eyes and his ruggedly handsome features. He had worn a white T-shirt and khaki cargo pants. And his big muscular frame had filled out both nicely. Well, nicely was too tame of a word. The guy had been unbelievably sexy. She couldn't help wondering how he looked out of those clothes.

Jennie sighed. She would never see him again, though. The only thing she knew about him was his first name, and that wasn't enough to find him. Why hadn't she given him her phone number? Or at least asked for his last name? But she just wasn't that forward. She had always let men pursue her instead of daring to pursue them, and look where that had gotten her. Divorced and lonely.

Well, if she ever saw Trevor again, she wouldn't make that mistake again. She would go after him. He would be worth it, of that she was certain.

∞∞∞

Jennie came awake, aching, and needy, small

glimpses from her dream still in her mind. Golden predatory eyes transitioning into warm brown ones. Large hands cupping and kneading her breasts. The feel of a muscular, hard chest against her hands.

She reached down with one hand into her panties and touched her clit. Imagining it was Trevor touching her, she used moisture from her wet pussy to coat her already swollen nub. She rubbed and pinched her clit. It didn't take long for her to climax, and she gasped as the orgasm rolled through her.

When her breathing settled down, she got out of bed. It was still early, but she felt rested and ready for a new day.

Jennie had a quick shower and went downstairs to the hotel restaurant to get some breakfast. Marna and Carlos were sitting at a large table, and she went over to join them.

"God morning, Jennie. Did you sleep well?" Marna was smiling at her, and Carlos nodded and smiled as well.

"Yes, I'm ready to tackle the world today, or at least Scotland." Jennie chuckled. "Isn't this the home of rugby or something? I wouldn't mind meeting one of those big rugby players. It might be fun letting him tackle me to the floor."

Jennie sobered when she noticed Marna gaping at her. Perhaps she was being a bit graphic, but Marna didn't usually have a problem with that.

Carlos was looking at her with a confused expression. "What about Michael?"

Feeling confused, Jennie stared at him. "What about him?"

"I don't think he would like you talking about other

men that way."

Jennie's jaw dropped. *What the hell?* "Why on earth does that have anything to do with him?"

"But I thought…" Carlos looked from her to Marna before fixing his gaze on her. "I thought you liked him and that this trip might help you guys get together. I know Michael likes you."

Jennie just shook her head slowly while contemplating what Carlos was saying. Was that why Michael was there, because he liked her? Did they really think she would fall for him? She had thought her friends knew her better than that. Feelings of betrayal and hurt gathered as a knot in her stomach.

She looked at Marna. "Is that why you invited me, to get together with Michael?"

Her friend shook her head firmly. "No, we invited you first. The idea of asking Michael to come along came later. He's a single, good-looking guy, and he's an old friend of Carlos and James. We thought you guys might hit it off."

Jennie didn't know what to say for a minute. She still felt hurt that they had set her up like that, but at least they hadn't invited her as a possible love interest for Michael. If anything, it was the other way around, which almost made her feel bad for him.

"What did you tell Michael about me when you invited him?"

Marna looked at Carlos, and he turned to Jennie. "I thought you liked him, so that's what I told him. Michael didn't even need time to think about it before he said yes. He really has a thing for you."

Jennie groaned in disbelief, but Marna spoke before she had a chance to respond. "I'm sorry we didn't tell you we asked him to come. I realize that was presumptuous and high-handed."

Jennie took a deep breath. "You should've asked me what I think of Michael first, before telling him that I like him." The hurt she felt was evident in her voice, but she couldn't help it. "To be blunt, I think he's a pompous ass. I've made a conscious effort to avoid him whenever I've seen him at a party. Whenever he opens his mouth, something arrogant or degrading comes out, and I can't stand it. To sum it up, my attraction to him is less than zero. He'd need a personality change for me to like him."

Carlos looked shocked at her candid speech, while Marna looked a bit ashamed.

"I'm sorry, Jennie, I didn't realize you'd had that much interaction with him and that you felt that way. Of course, we don't expect you to spend time alone with him if you don't like him. We're going to be together all six of us most of the time, anyway, so we'll make sure it doesn't ruin your vacation."

Jennie smiled. "It's okay, Marna. I'm sure he's already gotten the message that I'm not into him. And if he hasn't and he comes on to me, I'll tell him to back off in no uncertain terms."

Marna widened her eyes at her and nodded to her left. When Jennie turned her head to look, Michael, Ann, and James were heading toward their table.

Jennie pasted a huge smile on her face. "Good morning." Then she got up from the table. "I'll go grab something from the breakfast buffet."

***

Michael wanted to follow Jennie to the buffet table, but he stopped himself. He really needed to rethink how he approached her. Last night he thought she would be pleased that he had cared enough to order for her, but instead she had berated him for assuming to know what she wanted. It had taken him a while to get over the shock and acknowledge the fact that he really didn't know what she wanted. In fact, everything he did only seemed to annoy her.

There was only one thing left to do. He had to pretend to be one of those spineless men who talked to women like they were their best friends. It really went against everything he had been taught, but if that was the way to get Jennie to fall in love with him, he would do it. James and Carlos had reduced themselves to pussies to get their women, and it had obviously worked. What confused Michael was that his friends had continued their charades after securing their partners. It was like they had forgotten how to be real men.

Well, that wasn't going to happen to Michael. Once Jennie was his woman, he would revert to his manly behavior and show her how lucky she was. She would be able to rely on him to provide for her and make the important decisions, and she could spend her days doing whatever she liked. There would be no need for her to work another day in her life. She would show her gratitude in bed, and he would enjoy that magnificent body of hers every night.

ထထထ

Jennie relaxed into the seat on the train. They were on their way to Fearolc, and it made her think of Trevor. She recalled the astonished look on his face when she said where they were going. She got the feeling he knew the place more intimately than he let on. And the warning about not venturing outside after dark… Was it really because of the rough terrain? Jennie didn't think that was the only reason. There was something else behind that warning.

"A penny for your thoughts."

Jennie jumped at Ann's voice breaking through her reverie. They were seated together, and the rest of their party had seats a bit farther down the carriage.

"Oh, just thinking about the place we're going to stay, wondering what it's like." That wasn't a lie, even if it was only a part of what she had been thinking about. "How did you end up choosing Fearolc?"

"Purely by chance really." Ann sipped the coffee she had bought. "We searched for an apartment or cottage to rent in the Highlands, and we fell for the cute little cottage in Fearolc. It is remote and romantic, and there are plenty of hiking trails in the area. I really hope the pictures weren't lying."

"Yeah, me too. I look forward to being able to unpack and settle in one place for a few days."

"We haven't discussed who's going to have which room yet, though. I hope it won't be a problem." Ann sighed.

"What do you mean?" Jennie felt a bit apprehensive. They had told her there were four bedrooms in the cottage. Hopefully, they were all still available. If something had happened and she had to share with Michael, that would be a problem.

"There are three bedrooms in one end of the house, then there is the living room, kitchen, and bathroom in the middle, and in the other end there is another bedroom. There's a catch with the last bedroom, though. It's not accessible from inside the house but has its own entrance outside. I don't know if anyone wants to stay there."

Jennie's relief made her laugh. "Don't worry. I'll be happy to stay there." She lowered her voice. "For a minute there, I thought you were going to tell me I'd have to share a bedroom with Michael."

Ann's worried expression turned amused, and she chuckled. "We wouldn't have done that to you, although it would've been fun to see your expression when I told you that you had to share with him. I'm sorry we assumed you might like him. Marna told me what you said this morning. We should've asked you."

Jennie shook her head, smiling. "It's okay. Don't worry about it." The shock of finding out why they had asked Michael to come had passed, and she wasn't going to let that prick ruin her vacation.

After a while she went to the bathroom and when she came back, Ann was gone, and Michael was sitting in the seat Ann had vacated. Jennie didn't feel like talking to him, but they were going to share a cottage for a week, so she would have to try to treat him with respect, even if he didn't return the favor.

She sat down and decided to try to be polite and nice to him like she would be to any other person. "What do you think about the scenery so far? Beautiful, isn't it?"

"I guess. It doesn't compare to you, though." His tone was pleasant, and when she turned to gape at him, he looked back at her with a serious expression.

Jennie was so stunned by his compliment that she had to swallow a couple of times before getting her voice to function again. "Thank you." She tried to come up with something more to say, but her mind was completely blank.

"I wouldn't mind if you shared my room at the cottage. Then you don't have to stay in the separate room outside."

She studied him, but there was nothing on his face to indicate he meant it as a come-on. He was looking at her with something like careful hope in his eyes, and she realized he might actually have real feelings for her, even though he had been an ass about showing them to her so far.

"Um, that's considerate of you, but I don't mind staying in that room. Besides, we don't really know each other that well. I'd feel awkward staying in the same bedroom as you." And she didn't want to give him any reason to believe she was attracted to him.

"Okay, I don't want you to feel awkward. Do you want me to stay in the separate room so you can have a room inside?"

Talk about a personality transplant. If Michael hadn't been directly in front of her eyes, Jennie wouldn't have believed it was the same guy who scolded the mother of a young child the day before.

"No, I'll be fine in the separate room. But thank you for asking." Jennie gave him a genuine smile. "Have you been to Scotland before?"

He nodded. "Yes, but not the west coast. I've been to Edinburgh and Aberdeen. Business, though, not pleasure. I didn't have time to see much outside of the office."

"Michael?" They both looked up to see Marna standing in the aisle. "Do you mind if we switch places? I'd like to talk to Jennie about something."

"Not at all." He got up and turned to Jennie with a smile. "I'll talk to you later." Then, he made his way down the aisle to the others.

Marna sat down and looked at her. "I thought you might need a break from him," she whispered. "He insisted that Ann switch seats with him, and she felt bad for not being able to talk him out of it without making a scene."

"Normally, I would, but I think he might've had a brain transplant overnight or something. He was actually being polite and nice like a normal person. It's almost enough to make me wonder if it's all an act to make me fall for him."

Marna stared at her with amusement shining in her eyes. "Suspicious much? Maybe you guys just got off on the wrong foot before."

"Perhaps. We'll see if he keeps it up. I'm not holding my breath."

CHAPTER 4

They spent the rest of the train ride talking and looking out the window, enjoying the scenery, and the hours flew by. The Highlands were even more wild and beautiful than Jennie had imagined, and when she glimpsed a magnificent specimen of Scottish red deer with huge antlers, a sense of joy bubbled through her body. No matter what happened after this moment, this trip had already been worth it.

Fearolc turned out to be a tiny village. There were only about thirty houses altogether. A few trees were spread in and around the village, and not far behind it, the rocky hills were rising, covered in grass and shrubbery. It was beautiful, set on the shore of a sea loch, and Jennie found herself immediately enamored by the place. She couldn't wait to start exploring.

The cottage was cozy and rustic, situated at the end of a short driveway. It was invisible from the main road, located within a small grove of trees. A picnic table was placed by the south end of the house, which afforded small glimpses of the sea loch through the foliage.

The rooms were clean and nicely decorated in light colors, and the dark wooden beams in the ceiling and the broad, dark floorboards gave the cottage an authentic and homey feel.

Jennie's room was located in the southern end of the building, and the entrance was around the corner from the door to the rest of the house. The room was quite big with a queen-size bed, a tall bureau with eight drawers, and a small desk. She placed her big suitcase on the floor and started unpacking.

Even though she had brought a lot of clothes and shoes, it didn't take her long to unpack. Jennie placed the empty suitcase in the corner and grabbed her backpack. She took out her laptop, placed it on the small desk, and then plugged it in to charge. Thankfully, she had remembered to buy a power plug adapter at the airport.

Jennie heard someone approaching outside. She had left the door to her room open, and Ann walked in. "We're going to have a look around the village and then get some groceries on our way back. Do you want to come?"

"Do you mind if I stay here? I've got a bit of a headache and thought I'd just lie down for a little while." It was the truth, kind of. She did have a slight headache, but she didn't actually plan to lie down.

"No problem. We'll see you when we get back then." Ann smiled and left.

A couple of minutes later, she heard them talking as they walked away. Jennie had a look around the corner to see who was going, even though she felt a bit like she was spying on them. All five of them were walking down the driveway toward the main road, and she breathed a sigh of relief. Michael had gone with them, so he wouldn't be bothering her while the others were away.

Jennie turned to look toward the water and noticed a path in between the trees. She followed it until it emerged from the trees on the rocky shore of the sea loch. After moving all the way out onto the rocks by the water's edge, she stood there, taking it all in. It was fascinating. The water was so clear she could see fish almost a foot long swimming around, and even though she had never been pole fishing before in her life, she suddenly felt like trying it.

"Are you hungry?"

She started at the sound of the deep voice behind her, and her right foot slid off the rock she was standing on. Jennie could feel her body tilting toward the water, and there was nothing she could grab onto to prevent her from falling in.

A pair of strong arms wrapped around her waist, and she was yanked back and turned to end up pressed face-first tightly against the front of a very muscular man.

"Easy there, Jennie. I didn't mean to startle you." The dark voice sending vibrations from her ear throughout her whole body could only belong to one man.

"Trevor?" She pushed at his chest, and he loosened his hold on her enough to let her lift her head and stare into his beautiful brown eyes. They were filled with warmth and amusement.

"You should be careful on these rocks. They can be

quite slippery."

She narrowed her eyes at him in mock indignation. "It wouldn't have been a problem if someone hadn't tried to scare me to death."

Trevor threw his head back and laughed, and it was probably the most erotic sound she had ever heard. Her nipples tightened instantly. Then, he looked back down at her with eyes shining with amusement. "Fair enough, but I wasn't kidding about the rocks being slippery, and the next time I might not be here to save you from getting wet."

They both seemed to realize the double meaning of his words at the same time, and Jennie couldn't help it when her eyes dipped to his mouth. He had wide, full lips that looked both firm and soft, even though that seemed like a contradiction. She could think of several places on her body where she would like to feel those lips.

***

Trevor was struggling not to give in to his urge to kiss Jennie. They had just met and knew nothing about each other. It was too early to even think about kissing her, but that did nothing to stop his body from anticipating a lot more action than kissing. The feel of her in his arms and her breasts pressed against his chest didn't help either. Jennie pulled her lower lip into her mouth and sucked on it, and he felt his cock stir. Just the thought of what her mouth could do to him had his blood flowing south.

He quickly released Jennie and took a step to the side before she could feel what she was doing to him. Keeping one arm on her waist to support her, he led her off the rocks and back to the trees.

"So, you're staying at the Miller's cottage then?" Trevor glanced at her, before he let go of her waist and sat down next to a large tree.

She smiled at him and sat down facing him. "If you mean the cottage back there through the trees?" She pointed. "Then, yes. We just arrived about an hour ago. You didn't tell me you were staying here as well."

He debated what to tell her but decided to tell her the truth. "I've got a house here. I guess you could call it my second home."

Jennie widened her eyes in surprise. "You live here? I can understand why. It's beautiful here. You don't sound like you grew up here, though."

"No, I grew up in America, and I live there, but my house here has been in my family for generations. I visit often. It's quiet and relaxing."

"Yes." Jennie got a longing look in her eyes and a touch of sadness that he didn't like seeing there. "I wouldn't mind living a place like this, away from all the craziness of the world."

And he wouldn't mind living in a place like this with her. The realization startled him. He had never felt the need to settle down before. Lovers came and went, and he had felt comfortable not being tied down to one person. And then there was the fact that they weren't even the same species. He was a werewolf, and mating a human was frowned upon, even more so since he was an alpha. He didn't have a pack, but it was expected of him to take on that responsibility soon, and then he needed an alpha female by his side.

"Do you want me to take you back to the cottage?" Trevor stood and reached out to Jennie to help her up.

Jennie frowned but let him have her hand to pull

her to her feet. "No, I'll be fine. I'll just follow the path through the trees."

"Okay, maybe I'll see you later then." He let go of her hand and gave her a warm smile. Then, he gave her a short nod, turned, and walked away from her.

Every fiber in his being was screaming at him to go back to her, but that was just more of a reason to stay away. He had never met anyone that affected him the way she did, but he couldn't have her. Trevor realized that even having her as a lover would be impossible. He would grow too attached to her and would never be able to let her go.

His strong attraction to Jennie had caught him completely off guard. Perhaps it was because he had put off finding a mate for so long his body was suddenly trying to make it happen. But that couldn't be it either, since she wasn't a wolf. His body should have picked a wolf and not a human.

***

Jennie watched Trevor's back as he walked away. What the hell had just happened? One minute he seemed to like her, and the next he couldn't get away from her fast enough. Was it something she said that had him running? Jennie thought about what she had told him, but she couldn't remember saying anything that had the potential to scare him away.

Letting out a deep breath, she started up the path toward the cottage. Men—they were impossible to understand. People kept saying that about women, but in her opinion, it applied just as well to men. The minute you thought you had them figured out, they did something unexpected, and you were back to square one. Maybe she should just give up on them altogether.

Jennie arrived at the cottage and walked into her room. She grabbed her laptop and went to sit at the picnic table outside. At least in her novels, she got to decide the course of the story and the thoughts and actions of the people involved. Well, mostly. Her characters tended to take on a life of their own, and the story seldom went in the direction Jennie thought it would when she started writing.

A while later she heard voices from the driveway. When she glanced over her shoulder, she saw her friends walking toward her with bags of groceries in their hands. She saved her work and closed down her laptop before getting up.

"Hey, Jennie, we talked to some of the locals and found something fun to do the day after tomorrow." Ann sounded really excited.

"Kayaking," Marna blurted out.

Ann scowled at her. "I was just getting to that."

Jennie laughed. Sometimes they acted like small children.

"That sounds great. I hope they have wetsuits we can borrow. I've got a feeling I'll need one." Jennie didn't mind getting wet, but she didn't like getting cold.

"They have wetsuits." Michael was smiling at her. "And they'll give us a short lesson to get us started."

"That sounds perfect." Jennie smiled back at him.

"Let's go make some dinner. I'm starving." Ann headed toward the cottage, and the rest of them followed.

They ate dinner at the picnic table outside and discussed which hiking trails were the best in the area.

They had picked up a map at the store showing all the trails in the area, both coastal walks and paths going through the hills. There were several to choose from, and even more if they caught the train for half an hour. Jennie had a feeling time would fly while staying there, and she would miss this place when she left.

CHAPTER 5

"What's with the brooding?" Duncan looked at him. "A new lover giving you a headache?"

"Not a lover." Trevor realized that he had been sitting at the kitchen table, thinking about what to do about Jennie for quite a while.

Duncan chuckled. "Ah, soon-to-be lover then."

Trevor looked at him and shook his head. "No, that wouldn't be a good idea."

Duncan's eyes widened in surprise. "That serious, huh?"

"She's human. I can't risk it."

"Then find another lover and ride it out of your system. That usually works."

"Perhaps I'll go up north for a few days. I haven't been there for years."

Duncan shrugged and grinned. "Why not just stay here? You just arrived, and there are plenty of activities to occupy your time around here. I can write you a list."

Trevor took a deep breath and let it out slowly. "I'd risk running into her, or even worse I'd go looking for her."

Duncan barked out a laugh. "She's here?" Then he seemed to realize something. "That's why you wanted to know who was renting out a house around here. When did you meet her?"

"On the plane and then at the airport. Some asshole stole her purse, and I knocked him out to get it back for her."

"And I bet she was really grateful." Duncan's eyes were filled with amusement. "You should've just fucked her and gotten it out of your system. Then you wouldn't have been thinking about her now."

Trevor didn't like to hear Duncan talking about Jennie that way. It didn't sit well with him. "Jennie's not like that. She deserves better. I don't think she's a one-night stand kind of woman."

"I hate to break it to your old-fashioned ass, but a lot of these modern women like one-night stands just as much as any man. It's called gender equality or some shit."

The growl left Trevor's throat before he could stop it. "Not Jennie!"

Duncan's eyes widened, and he raised his hands in the air. "Calm down. I'm not going to try my luck with her, all right? Are you sure she's not your mate? I've never seen you act like this over a woman before, and one you haven't even fucked yet at that. You have it bad."

Trevor groaned and buried his face in his hands. "I know. I'm sorry. Fuck! I can't have her, though. I need to mate an alpha female. But the thought of someone else having her makes my blood boil."

"Why don't you go for a run? I'll clean up here." Duncan got up and started clearing off the table.

"Thank you. Maybe using some energy will help me forget about her." Trevor didn't think it would be that easy, though. His attraction to Jennie was much stronger than he had first thought. Could it really be possible that she was his mate? That would explain his extreme possessiveness. But she wasn't a wolf, and he had thought that those kinds of feelings were reserved for wolf mates.

Perhaps he should pay Hamish and Ildri a visit in the morning. Hamish had mated Ildri a few years ago, even though she was human. Maybe he could tell Trevor what a mating between a wolf and a human was like, if it was as powerful a bond as was common between two wolves, or more like a human marriage. He would still have to stay away from Jennie, but at least he would know. Regardless, it was information that was useful when he decided to take on the responsibility of a pack.

It was dark outside, and he undressed just outside the back door before shifting into his wolf form. Immediately, his sense of smell and hearing improved, and he could hear all the small and large animals nearby. His cattle and sheep in the fields beyond the stone fence surrounding his lawn, small rodents in the grass, and birds in the trees. No foreign smells disturbed his senses, and he took off across the lawn to check his land and the surrounding mountains.

It gave him an amazing sense of freedom running around his large property. Few people ventured up into the hills at night, so the risk of running into someone was small. He occasionally met one of the local werewolves on his nightly runs, but that was it.

Duncan was doing well taking care of Trevor's property. He was a wolf as well, and they had met in America many years ago. Duncan was originally from Scotland and after many years of staying abroad he wanted to go back home to live. Taking care of Trevor's property was the perfect opportunity and suited them both well.

Trevor stopped when he suddenly realized where he was. He was standing amongst the trees by the Miller's cottage. It hadn't been his intention to go near that cottage again, but somehow, he had ended up there, anyway.

He carefully made his way to the other end of the cottage while staying amongst the trees. There were no lights on inside, and everything was quiet. He crept a little closer and used his nose to take in the scents in the area. Jennie's scent was easy to recognize, and it was strongest by the entrance at the south end of the cottage. There were quite a few other people who had been at the cottage in the last few days, but there were only five apart from Jennie that he didn't recognize as local people. Of those five, two were female, and three were male.

There was something a little off about the male scents, but he couldn't tell what was different about them. Were the males shifters of some kind? Trevor didn't know this particular scent element, though, so he couldn't be sure. That was strange, since he normally could tell from a person's scent if he or she was a shifter and which kind.

Trevor didn't like it, and he felt his hackles rising.

Jennie was living with people whom he didn't know anything about. He felt a strong urge to knock on the door and find out precisely what these people were right then, but he beat the feeling down. It wouldn't exactly endear him to Jennie, knocking on their door and demanding answers in the middle of the night. Completely nude, no less, since he hadn't brought any clothes.

If he could swear in wolf form, he would have. There was nothing else for him to do than to go home. These people were Jennie's friends and presumably she knew them well. So, most likely none of them posed any danger to her. But, it hadn't escaped his attention that there were three males and two females in addition to Jennie. The other two females' scents were laced with two of the males' scents, so they were most likely mated pairs. Did the last male have an interest in Jennie? Trevor knew she wasn't mated, and she hadn't been intimate with a male for a while. He would have been able to pick that up when she was close to him, even though his sense of smell was less developed in his human form. But just the fact that she might be staying in the same house as a male who wanted her had his blood boiling again.

Trevor crept silently back under the cover of the trees. He had to get out of there before he did something he would regret.

ꝏꝏꝏ

Jennie woke early. After getting out of bed, she dressed in a white T-shirt and blue shorts. The shorts were cool linen and reached to mid-thigh. She was looking forward to the day. They had decided on a nice coastal walk going north. Apparently, there were small white sand beaches to be found tucked in between the long stretches of rocky shoreline. They would bring their bathing suits and perhaps go for a swim. She wasn't quite sure about that last part, since the water was supposed to be cold around there, but if the sun got to work, it might be possible.

It was only seven in the morning, and Jennie had showered and shaved her legs before going to bed the night before. She opened her laptop and sat down to write for a while. The others wouldn't get up for another hour or two, so it was a bit early to start making breakfast.

At half past eight, she saved her work and closed her laptop. Her novel was coming along nicely. It was fun being privy to the main characters' interactions and the ups and downs of their developing relationship, all the while knowing that it would turn out well in the end. Jennie loved happy endings, so that was guaranteed in her stories.

In life, on the other hand, there were no such guarantees, as she had bitterly found out. She had met Olivier when she was twenty. He was dark and mysterious and the perfect gentleman. As she was quite inexperienced with men, he had swept her off her feet. And when she was twenty-one, he asked her to marry him. She had been ecstatic, and they had a small affordable wedding with just their closest friends two months later. Both hers and Olivier's parents were dead, so they didn't bother inviting any family.

She had felt extremely lucky, and for the first couple of years, she had lived a dream life. The perfect husband and enough money to lead an ordinary life without having to worry about anything. They lived in her old family home, which she had inherited when her parents died, and even though they weren't rich, she could get away with working a part-time job while spending the rest of her time focusing on her writing. She was happy and thought it would stay that way forever.

But after two years of marriage, Olivier started spending more and more time away from home. He told her it was work-related and that by putting in the extra hours, he was on his way to earning a big promotion, securing their future, and allowing Jennie to take time off to be a mom. It sounded perfect, and knowing he was doing it all for them to have a family, she didn't complain about his frequent absences.

That all changed when she received a phone call from Marna, asking her what was going on. Marna had seen Olivier leaving an expensive restaurant with a woman the night before, and they looked far more friendly than coworkers or friends should be. Olivier and the woman had gotten into a limousine and left, before Marna had been able to get his attention.

Olivier had told her not to wait up for him the day before. He was going to work on a project, and it would probably be past midnight by the time he was finished. He would just sleep in his office, something he had been doing regularly for the past three months.

Jennie didn't really want to believe he was cheating on her. He was so loving and perfect when they were together, even though that wasn't as often as it used to be. But she couldn't let it slide.

She contacted one of his co-workers that she had

met several times in the past couple of years. Asking the man about Olivier's projects confirmed her suspicions. Her husband wasn't working on anything important that demanded extra hours. On the contrary, he was on probation at work because his performance wasn't up to par. If he didn't improve soon, he would get fired.

Jennie confronted Olivier that night, and he admitted everything. The woman he was seen with leaving the restaurant was the sole heir of a wealthy family, and they were going to get married. He had been about to tell Jennie since he needed a divorce. Olivier had never loved her. He had married her because she had a house, and she was a good stepping stone for him to move up in life.

Her life fell apart, and if it hadn't been for Ann and Marna those first couple of months, Jennie wasn't sure how she would have been able to keep going. She'd had what she thought was the perfect life with the perfect husband, but it had all been a lie.

The divorce came through quickly due to the nature of the case, and two months after she had confronted Olivier, Jennie broke out of her misery and became angry. She found out who Olivier was going to marry and went to see the woman. The heiress wasn't sure if she wanted to let Jennie into her house at first, but Jennie managed to convince her. She told the woman everything, about how loving Olivier had been the years they had been together right up to the day she had found out he was cheating, and about how he was setting the woman up the same way he had set Jennie up. His only focus was to move up in the world, and he would do anything to get there.

In the end the heiress thanked her. Olivier was an amazing con man, and she would have been his second victim if Jennie hadn't told her what was going on.

After that Jennie hadn't seen or heard from Olivier ever again. She had expected him to come by and tell her off for ruining his chances with the other woman, but he never did. He probably cut his losses and moved somewhere else, which was perfect because if she never laid eyes on him again, it would be too soon.

Jennie exited her room and went to the kitchen. The house was still quiet, and none of her friends appeared to be up yet. But as she was starting to get hungry, Jennie got to work making breakfast. A couple of minutes later, she heard someone moving in the living room, and she turned around to see Michael coming into the kitchen.

"Good morning." She smiled at him. Hopefully, he was going to continue his behavior from the day before and be nice to her.

"Good morning." He smiled back, the smile reaching his eyes. "I'll help you make breakfast."

"Great, thank you. I'm not sure when the others will be up, but I'm hungry."

Michael chuckled. "Yeah, me to. Did you sleep well?"

"Yes, like a log. I don't even think I dreamed, at least not anything I can remember."

"You usually dream every night?" Michael looked at her curiously.

"Yes, don't you?"

He shook his head. "I don't think so, or perhaps I just can't recall any of it in the morning."

"Maybe it's just my creative mind that can't stop working, even at night." Jennie threw him a smile. "I always have a few stories developing in my head. It never stops."

"Do you manage to write everything down?" He had stopped what he was doing and was studying her face like he was trying to memorize it.

"No, I go with the story I think is best at the time. Sometimes I even write two novels at the same time. But there's plenty of ideas I discard or just don't have time to focus on. The bottle neck for me isn't coming up with ideas but finding time to write them out and develop the stories."

Michael smiled and took a step toward her, and she found herself freezing to the spot, hoping he wasn't going to try anything. She had already told him she wasn't his woman, but she wasn't certain what he had understood by that. Jennie had meant that he didn't have a chance with her. That she wasn't interested and never would be. But he might have thought she meant that she wasn't his woman yet, and that he might have a chance if he played his cards right.

Thankfully, Michael stopped and turned back to what he had been doing, and Jennie breathed a sigh of relief. She wasn't sure what had showed on her face when he had stepped toward her. It could have been anything from panic to distaste. Hopefully, it wasn't the last one. She didn't want to hurt Michael, even if she had no intention of accepting any advances from him.

"Ah, breakfast." Ann came into the kitchen, smiling. "You guys are so good."

Jennie smiled at her. She felt relieved at seeing her

friend. The silence between her and Michael was starting to feel awkward.

"Sit down. Everything is ready." Jennie put the rest of the food on the table, and as she sat down, Marna, Carlos, and James walked into the kitchen as well.

"Ah, food." James took a seat next to Ann.

Jennie chuckled. "You sound just like your wife. Even if I didn't know you guys were married, the way you talk would've clued me in quickly. And of course, the fact that you always seem to be touching each other. Don't get me wrong. It's cute."

"Cute." James scowled at her, while Ann started laughing.

They ate, talked, and laughed. Jennie relaxed and enjoyed herself. It was nice being around Ann and Marna again, even if they were all lovey-dovey with their husbands. Actually, it was nice seeing the love between the couples. It seemed so genuine that it almost made her believe she could find love again herself.

Or perhaps again was the wrong word to use. She was coming to realize what she had with Olivier had never been love. He had always been so perfect and done everything to please her. Even when he started staying away more, he made sure that the reason he gave for doing so was for their life to be even more perfect. She had been in love with the idea of the perfect husband and the perfect family, but she wasn't sure she had actually loved Olivier the man. Jennie had mourned the loss of the perfect life they'd had, but she hadn't missed him as a person.

And if she was going to be really honest with herself, their love life had been boring and repetitive, but she had thought that was what happened with married couples after a little while. Seeing how her friends were acting around their husbands, though, made her realize it didn't have to be like that. There was a spark in her friends' marriages that hadn't been there in hers.

They cleaned up after breakfast before getting ready for their coastal walk. Jennie went back to her room and found her sunscreen lotion. She made sure to apply it all over. Otherwise, with her pale skin, it wouldn't take more than half an hour in the sun before she resembled a tomato.

She put her new bikini, towel, and sunscreen in her backpack, and after adding her packed lunch and water bottle, she was ready to go. After locking the door to her room, she put the key in her pocket before walking around the corner to join the others.

CHAPTER 6

Trevor wanted to go visit Jennie, but he was trying to talk himself out of it. It wasn't a good idea to call on her. The more time he spent with her, the more difficult it would be to let her go. He had thought about going to see Hamish and Ildri to find out about their mating bond, but it was better to wait until Jennie had left. If he found out that a wolf and a human could form a strong mating bond, he would be even more tempted to pursue her.

Another reason he wanted to go visit Jennie was to meet her friends. He wanted to know what kind of shifters they were. Trevor was quite sure they were shifters. He couldn't think of anything else they could be. But did they realize they were in the middle of wolf country?

Different kinds of shifters tended to stay away from each other, since most of them were quite territorial and didn't like others inside what they considered their area. It could even be an issue between different packs or clowders of the same shifter kind.

If Jennie's friends hadn't shifted in the area yet, they might not have picked up the scents of all the wolves around there. They were in for a surprise when they did, or if they did. But that was the risk you ran when you were traveling as a shifter. You might end up in someone's territory without realizing it.

Trevor gave up. He had to see Jennie just to make sure she was all right and not being pressured into something she didn't want. He hated the fact that there was an unmated male shifter in that cottage with her.

Running down toward the sea loch and the cottage, he tried to calm the rage that simmered within him. He had no right to get angry just because someone else might be interested in Jennie, but he couldn't help it. She meant something to him.

He slowed when he got to the driveway and focused on walking at a normal speed. Acting like a lunatic sprinting up to the cottage and demanding answers wasn't the way to go.

The cottage seemed quiet and deserted, and knocking on the door didn't provoke any response. He walked around to the south end of the cottage and knocked on the door there as well, but there was still no response. They were obviously out, perhaps for the whole day. There were plenty of trails around this area, mostly used by the locals. But there were a few tourists that went there for the day just to follow one of the trails.

Trevor wanted to shift so he could follow their scents to wherever they were. She was out walking with some unmated asshole that might be trying to get into her pants, or even worse, trying to lure her into becoming his mate.

A thought popped into his mind. Did Jennie know that the males were shifters? Obviously, the other human females did since they were mated to them, but what about Jennie? Shifters weren't supposed to tell humans about their existence. It could lead to a lot of problems. There was already enough racism and religious conflicts in the world without adding shifters into the mix. Shifters were stronger and lived longer than humans, and that would lead to jealousy, and nothing good ever came of jealousy.

His guess would be that Jennie didn't know about her friends being shifters, but he could be wrong. Maybe he should try finding out. If nothing else, he should warn her friends that they were living among wolves.

∞∞∞

Jennie loved the sea and the view of the islands covering the horizon. They were walking along the rocky shore with occasional breaks while passing through small groves of trees. It was a beautiful, warm day, and the sun beating down on their heads might have felt too hot if not for the constant cool breeze fanning them.

Michael had come up behind Jennie a few minutes ago and was currently walking beside her. He hadn't said anything yet, so she found herself being unsure of what to expect. But she wasn't going to let him ruin her great experience no matter what kind of mood he was in.

She sighed happily. "It's so beautiful here. This is the kind of place where I could see myself settling down. Sitting in the shade by the sea somewhere with my laptop and a cool drink. It would be heaven."

"Don't you like the city?" Michael's voice sounded a bit surprised. "I had you pegged as a city girl."

"No, not really. Sure, there's always something happening, and everything is within a few minutes' drive, but I prefer peace and quiet. I'd rather live somewhere remote like this."

"I'd hate living here. There's nothing to do." He sounded annoyed.

Jennie chuckled. "Well, we're doing something right now. Isn't this nice?"

Michael didn't answer, and she turned to look at him. He looked angry and didn't meet her gaze.

She turned back to the scenery and decided to leave him to stew in his anger. Whatever had him in such a mood wasn't her problem.

Her thoughts turned to Trevor. She wished he was walking alongside her instead. He would have taken her hand, helped her over the rocky outcrops, and saved her if she tripped.

He would have been a distraction, though, with his beautiful brown eyes and his amazing physique. If she tripped, it would probably be because she was staring at his tight, muscular ass or forgot where she was because he took off his shirt.

Jennie still didn't understand what had happened the previous day. They had been talking and getting to know each other, and then he had suddenly been in a hurry to leave.

Perhaps she was just reading too much into it. He

had given her a warm smile before he left and hadn't appeared to be annoyed or angry in any way. He might just have remembered something he had to do.

"I'm sorry you don't like the city. I do, and I don't think I'd ever want to live anywhere else." Michael's glum voice startled her. He had been quiet for so long she had forgotten he was there.

"Well, we're different then, that's all. It doesn't matter." She tried to sound light and cheery to offset his somberness.

They were just emerging from a small cluster of trees and Jennie stopped, staring at what lay in front of them.

"Wow, look at that white sand." Jennie was in awe. The tiny beach was shining in the sunlight it was so white, and the water was clear and a light bottle-green close to the beach, turning into royal-blue farther out. "I think I might like to go for a swim. That water looks so clean even my thoughts will be pure by the time I get out."

"You have impure thoughts?"

Michael's question caught her off guard, and she turned to look at him before she could stop herself. He was studying her with a small knowing smile on his face, and she inwardly swore. She did have impure thoughts, but they were most definitely not about him.

"I don't think you should let your assumptions run away with you." Her voice was a bit sharper than she had intended, but she wanted to stop him thinking she had any interest in him.

Jennie turned away from him and walked down to the beach. Rummaging through her backpack, she found her bikini and her towel. She changed into her bikini while holding the towel around her, and when she was done, Ann and Marna walked up to her. They had been walking a little behind her and Michael.

"Are you going in?" Marna looked at her expectantly.

Jennie nodded and smiled. "Yes, the water looks amazing. I'm sure it's cold, but I have to try it."

Marna nodded enthusiastically. "Yes, me too. Wait for me, okay? I just have to change."

"Ann?" Jennie looked at her other friend. "Are you coming with us?"

Ann looked like she was debating it before nodding. "Yeah, I'd regret it if I didn't."

James and Carlos walked up as Ann and Marna were changing.

James lifted one eyebrow as he looked at his wife doubtfully. "It's going to be cold."

Ann smiled at him, trying to contain her amusement. "Yeah, but I can handle it. You should come with me."

James put a hand protectively over his groin. "I don't think so. My nuts would fall off, and my dick might never regain its current size. You like my big cock, so asking me to get in the water with you is not in your best interest."

Ann laughed. "You're so crude sometimes. I love you."

Jennie snorted. "Too much information. I'm going for a swim." She walked toward the water. Ann and Marna would follow as soon as they were finished changing.

The water was cold. Dipping her toes in, she debated whether this was a good idea or not.

"My nuts are waterproof, and the cold won't change the fact that I'm hung like a horse." Michael's words coming from her right had her whip her head around, ready to lay into him for being an arrogant bastard, but seeing the humor in his eyes and the way his mouth twitched with barely contained laugher stopped her short.

She narrowed her eyes at him. "Are you baiting me?"

His eyes widened, and he shook his head. "Just joking. I didn't mean anything by it. Please, I—"

Jennie burst out laughing. "I so got you."

Michael stood there, gaping at her and appeared to be unsure exactly how to react. She stopped laughing but couldn't keep the smile off her face.

He stepped forward quickly and before she realized what he intended, he kissed her right on her lips. Then, he turned and ran into the water a few steps before diving in, submerging his body completely.

She stood there stunned. Michael kissing her wasn't something she would have agreed to if he had asked, but she couldn't really fault him for trying his luck. She had sort of invited it by teasing him.

"What just happened?" Marna's whisper in her ear made her jump. "Sorry, I didn't mean to sneak up on you."

Jennie sighed. "Shit, I don't really know. We made a few jokes, and he suddenly kissed me. I didn't see it coming, or I'd have stopped it."

"How was it?"

Marna's question made Jennie turn to look at her. Her friend studied her curiously. "Awkward. I really hope he doesn't think that was the beginning of something."

Marna frowned. "You felt nothing. No spark at all?"

"Nope. I don't like him, remember? I want to have a good time while I'm here, though, so I'm trying to get along with him. We don't see eye to eye in a lot of things, but I'm trying to look away from that to enjoy my vacation. But if he kisses me again, I'll knee him in the groin."

"Maybe you should just be straight with him and tell him you don't like him that way."

Jennie sighed in frustration. "I feel like I've tried that several times already, but perhaps I've been too subtle. He's obviously not getting the message. But if I'm too crass, he might get pissed off, and that will ruin our vacation. I feel like I'm treading a fine line here."

Marna nodded. "I see what you mean."

Michael was swimming back toward them, and they needed to change the subject. Jennie looked at Marna and then back toward Ann, who was still on the beach having friendly banter with her husband.

"Well, it's now or never." Marna looked determined. "If I stay here any longer, I'll change my mind about this."

"Okay, let's go."

They wandered out into the cold water, and Jennie was sure she was going to lose the feeling in her legs. Michael was approaching them, but she purposefully avoided looking at him. She mentally prepared herself to tell him off if he came up to her, but he passed by them and made for the beach without saying anything or trying to get her attention.

Jennie breathed out a sigh of relief. At least that was something. Perhaps he finally understood she didn't like him or his advances.

Marna dived in and Jennie followed, surfacing after just a couple of strokes. She gasped as the cold water seemed to shrink her skin, causing a slight burning sensation. She'd had enough and turned around to go back to the beach, only to come face to face with Ann.

"You kissed him." Ann was whispering, even though they were well out of earshot of the guys, who were standing and talking on the beach. Her friend looked surprised and delighted at the same time, and Jennie frowned.

"He kissed me before I could stop him, and I didn't like it. I'll deck him if he ever does that again."

"Oh." Ann's excitement sobered, and she almost looked a bit sad.

Jennie suddenly felt like she was missing something. "I've already told you that I don't like Michael. Why do you still want me to get together with him?"

Ann looked at her with guilt visible in her eyes. "I'm sorry. I don't want you to do anything that doesn't feel right for you. It's just that he's James's friend. It would be sort of cool if you guys hit it off."

Jennie frowned and studied her friend. She got the feeling there was more to it than that, and it didn't feel good that her friend kept something hidden from her.

"To be precise, I don't like Michael. Even if he was the last man on earth, I wouldn't go for him. Please trust me on that."

Jennie stepped around Ann and walked toward the beach. She had never had any reason not to trust her friend before. Most people would probably say she was being paranoid, but she knew her friends. They had spent a lot of time together, and she knew their body language. There was something Ann wasn't telling her, and whether it was because she didn't want to or because she wasn't able to for some reason, it still hurt.

She quickly dried off before spreading her towel out on the sand and lying down on her back. The sun slowly heated her body, and it was so nice just lying there, basking in the rays of the sun, that it didn't take long before she drifted off to sleep.

CHAPTER 7

Angry voices shouting at each other woke Jennie up; a bit disoriented from sleep, she sat up and looked around. The sun didn't appear to have moved much, so she couldn't have been asleep for long.

Turning around, she took in the scene that was playing out behind her. Three men she had never laid eyes on before were having an angry shouting match with James, Carlos, and Michael, and the aggressiveness of the strangers made her get up. What on earth was going on? James and Carlos were both easygoing guys who got along with everyone, so either Michael had managed to get on these guys' nerves, or the three strangers had caused whatever was happening.

Jennie approached slowly and carefully while trying to understand what was going on. James, Carlos, and Michael were standing face to face with the three strangers, with James a couple of steps in front of his friends like he was acting as their leader or spokesperson. Marna and Ann were standing a couple of yards behind their respective husbands.

"You pussies have no business being here." The tallest and brawniest stranger was staring daggers at James, and his whole body seemed tense like he was expecting her friends to attack at any moment. "This is our territory."

James stood his ground and didn't break eye contact with the stranger. "Like I said. We're not here to encroach on your territory. We're here on vacation with our wives."

"Well, we want you gone. Pack your shit and get out of here. This is wolf country."

Jennie froze. There were wolves in this area? That was news to her. Then it dawned on her that it was probably the name of a motorcycle club or something. There were no actual wolves around there.

"We'll be leaving on Saturday. Until then we're going to enjoy our vacation with our females." James kept his eyes locked with the tallest stranger and didn't back down, but he spoke calmly. "There is no reason for you to feel threatened by us."

"Threatened?" This appeared to really rile the guy up. "We can break you fuckers in two seconds flat. Why the fuck would we feel threatened? We just want you to show us some respect and leave. You don't fucking belong here."

Jennie didn't like the direction this was heading. The big stranger seemed to want a fight, and judging by his size and the size of his two friends, she wasn't sure that it would turn out in her friends' favor. James, Carlos, and Michael were all fit and muscular, but none of them were as big and brawny as the guys they were facing off with. The biggest of the strangers was almost as big and built as Trevor, and the other two were only marginally smaller.

James seemed to struggle to stay calm. "We've rented a cottage from George Miller, and we'll be staying there until Saturday. If you've got a problem with that, you should talk to George."

"George." The big guy spat on the ground after saying the name. "He has no say in who is welcome around here and will get what is coming to him. George's invitation for you to stay is hereby revoked, and it's time for you to leave." Taking a step forward, the guy was just a foot away from James, making the size difference between the two even more obvious.

Jennie had stopped a few yards away and wasn't sure what to do. She got the feeling that there were rules in this confrontation she didn't know, like the fact that only James and the guy directly in front of him spoke. The others all stood around them, backing them up, but they hadn't uttered one word while she had been listening. And the way Marna and Ann were positioned a few yards behind their respective husbands wasn't by accident. The women were showing whom they belonged to.

James stood his ground. "We've got no dispute with you, and we have no wish to fight. Our wives are present."

As if on cue, all the strangers turned their heads to look at Jennie. The way they looked at her made her feel like they were evaluating her place in all of this. She wasn't standing with her friends but more off to the side. Were they reading something into that?

She looked at her friends and met Michael's eyes.

He looked a bit worried and used his head to indicate she should get behind him. Jennie took a step toward him, but before she could take another step, a feeling of wrongness shot through her, and she stopped. She wasn't sure why she felt that way, but she decided to heed the feeling. Maybe it was because she didn't belong to Michael.

Looking back at the strangers, she noticed the guy in front of James narrow his eyes while studying her. Then he turned to look at James.

"You're traveling with an unmated female? Why would you do that?"

Jennie wasn't sure she had heard him correctly. Unmated female? And then to ask why she was traveling with them? What was this guy going on about? This was getting stranger by the second, but for some reason, her friends didn't appear surprised by the stranger's questions.

"She is a close friend of my wife's, but unaware of our status." James never turned to look at her but kept his eyes on the man facing him.

Jennie felt totally confused. What did James mean that she was unaware of their status? Did this have something to do with them wanting her to get together with Michael? Just the thought made her see red, and any fear of a possible fight between the guys disappeared.

She took a few steps toward the strangers, and the man who had asked questions about her turned his head toward her again.

"I'll have you know that I'm single by choice and nobody's property." Jennie stared into the stranger's eyes while she was talking. "There is no law against me, or any of my friends for that matter, traveling in this country. And I'd be happy to speak to the police if you make any more threats against any of us."

"Jennie!" Michael was stalking toward her, and he was obviously not happy with what she was saying. But she didn't care.

The stranger's eyes were narrow with anger. "You should stay out of this. This is not your fight. You can stay if you want to, but your friends here need to leave. Having George vouch for them isn't good enough."

Michael grabbed her upper arm and tried to pull her away from the men still facing James and Carlos. "Jennie, come with me."

Anger surged through her, and she really wanted to hit him, but instead she yanked her arm out of his grip. "Stay away. I don't need a babysitter."

Then, she suddenly realized what the stranger had said about having someone to vouch for them, and she turned to him and spoke before she could think better of it. "Do you know Trevor?"

The guy had been looking at James, but when she spoke, his eyes snapped to hers. He looked shocked. Several seconds went by before he spoke.

"You know Trevor?"

"Yes, he will vouch for us. He knows we're here." She sounded more confident than she felt. Jennie hoped she was right when she said Trevor would vouch for them.

The three strangers suddenly backed up several steps and looked like they wanted to bolt in fear. "Please accept our apologies. Enjoy your stay. We'll not bother you again." They turned and hurried away.

Jennie was stunned and didn't move until the

strangers were out of sight. She looked at her friends, and they were all staring at her.

She frowned. "What?"

James sucked in a deep breath before he spoke. "Trevor. Is that the guy from the airport?"

Jennie nodded. "Yes, he's the one who caught the thief who stole my purse."

"How did you know that he lives around here and knows those assholes?"

"He told me he has a house around here. It's a small community, so I assumed they would know him." But she had no idea why those men got so scared when she mentioned Trevor's name. It was a bit disturbing, actually. Trevor had seemed like such a nice guy, but there were obviously things she didn't know about him.

"Are you sure he would vouch for us?" James looked at her with a neutral expression on his face. She had no idea what he was thinking.

"No, but I told him where we were going, and he didn't tell me that we couldn't stay here."

James sighed and didn't appear convinced. "Well, he's obviously respected around here."

And there was that feeling again that there was something she didn't know, something that would make sense of what had just happened. It left her feeling like she was the odd one out in the group, and that she didn't really know her friends anymore. Even Michael appeared to be in on whatever this was, and she was left feeling alone.

"Let's go back to the cottage." James looked around, and they all nodded.

It was well past midday, and it was time to leave,

anyway. Jennie turned and looked at the beach and the water lapping gently at the shore. For some reason, it didn't look quite the same anymore. The beach and the sea were still beautiful, but it was like a dark cloud had moved in and obscured some of view. The sun was still shining, and there was no actual cloud, of course. It just felt like there were nuances to this place that were hidden from her but visible to everyone else.

Jennie changed back into her T-shirt and shorts and packed all her things in her backpack. She fell in behind the others as they made their way along the shore, back the way they had come. Nobody talked and it suited her fine. She didn't really feel like speaking to any of the others at the moment.

The way the strangers had acted when she mentioned Trevor's name was still bothering her. Why were they scared of him? It wasn't a feeling she associated with him at all. He was hot as hell, of course, and maybe she was a bit blinded by how protectively he had acted toward her, but it was hard to imagine him doing something so bad it would make grown men afraid of him.

The events at the airport suddenly replayed in her head. There had been too many people in between her and the thief for her to see everything that happened, but she remembered the guy flying to the right like he had been hit by a truck. And that truck had to have been Trevor. Was that why the strangers who had tried to intimidate them on the beach were scared of Trevor? He would come down on them like a ton of bricks if he heard what had happened to her and her friends? But three against one wasn't good odds for Trevor, so it still didn't make sense to Jennie. Unless

Trevor had people they knew would side with him. That had to be it. It was the only logical explanation.

"So, the guy from the airport is staying here?" Michael's voice right next to her made her jump.

She turning to look at his face, but it was impossible to judge his mood. His expression was passive and didn't give away what he was thinking.

"Yes, when I told him where we were going, he said he had a house in Fearolc." That was close enough to the truth. Jennie wasn't going to tell him she had met Trevor again last night.

"Do you know which house is his?" There were still no emotions showing on his face, and she had no idea why he was asking her these questions. Was it because he was wondering about the guy who commanded so much respect around there, or because he wanted to be prepared in case there was another incident like the one on the beach?

"No, I have no idea. I didn't talk to him for very long."

"And he didn't give you his phone number?"

Jennie shook her head. "No."

Michael nodded and looked straight ahead. He appeared to be content with her answers and didn't ask any more questions. He was clearly just trying to make sure they would be safe while staying there, and he wanted to know how to contact Trevor if something else happened.

***

Michael was satisfied with Jennie's answers. Even though the asshole at the airport seemed to have made an impression on her, there was no further attachment. He had been pissed off at first when he realized

Trevor was staying in the village, but he couldn't stay angry when the asshole's name had saved them from a fight with local wolves.

Wolves, there were fucking wolves in the area. He had no idea how many, but by the way the idiots at the beach had acted, there had to be more of them. And the way they had reacted on hearing Trevor's name, the bastard was clearly a wolf, as well, perhaps even their alpha.

If it were up to him, they would leave this place right this minute and find somewhere else to stay, but he was quite sure James would disagree. He seemed to have made up his mind about staying there, and there was no budging him if he had. James wasn't Michael's alpha, but he was more powerful and therefore by default in charge.

He glanced at Jennie walking beside him and wondered what she made of the altercation on the beach. Ann and Marna were fully aware of the shifter world and knew what to do when there was a dispute with other shifters, but Jennie had no idea what was going on. If she would just allow him to mate her, he would tell her everything. But until that happened, he had to be careful not to reveal their true nature, which left Jennie vulnerable while she was traveling with them. Unmated humans in the company of shifters were often considered fair game, so they needed to watch out for her more carefully while they were staying in this area.

"Perhaps we should switch rooms at the cottage. You'd be safer staying inside the house than outside in that room by yourself." Michael kept his eyes on her face while speaking to judge her reaction.

Jennie looked a bit taken aback. "Why, do you expect those guys to try to get us to leave again? They appeared to be scared when they left. I can't imagine they'll try again."

"It's just as a precaution."

She shook her head. "No, I'm not scared, and I'll be staying exactly where I am. I don't think they'll be back."

Michael wanted to argue his case but decided against it. She was most likely correct that the bastards wouldn't be back to annoy them, and he didn't want to get into another argument with Jennie.

"Okay, but please lock your door at night at least." A wolf wouldn't have any problem breaking down that door, but it would make a lot of noise and alert the rest of them to what was happening.

She nodded. "Okay."

***

On their way through the village, they stopped by the small grocery store. Jennie studied the two other customers in there, but they didn't seem hostile toward them in any way. When she smiled, they smiled back, and none of them appeared to have a problem with her group of friends. At least the whole village wasn't against them. It might have been just those three guys at the beach. Every town had their bad apples, and they might just have been unfortunate to run into them. A simple case of bad luck.

When they exited the store, it was much darker outside, and she looked up to see dark clouds coming in from the west and piling up like a mass of cotton candy. It would probably start raining later. Hopefully, it would blow over during the night and be nice again the next day.

CHAPTER 8

It was still a bit too early to make dinner when they got back to the cottage, and after taking a shower, Jennie went to her room to write for a little while. The others gathered in the living room with beers and snacks, but she felt a bit off after everything that had happened that day and really needed some time to herself.

She sat down at the small desk and fired up her laptop, but her mind kept reverting to their experience with the three men at the beach. No matter how much she tried, Jennie couldn't focus on the story she was writing. After half an hour, she gave up and shut down her laptop.

It hadn't started raining yet, so she put on some shoes and opened the door. The wind was starting to pick up, and the temperature had dropped, so she put on her jacket, as well, before walking outside and locking her door.

The short walk through the trees down to the rocky shore by the sea loch only took a couple of minutes.

When Jennie emerged from the trees, she was surprised at how the wind was whipping up the water to give the waves white crests of foam. It was powerful and a bit scary yet natural and awe-inspiring at the same time, and for some reason, she felt her edginess fade away and be replaced by a sense of calm. She stepped out onto the rocks, spread her arms out and raised her face to the sky, closing her eyes. The wind was tugging hard at her clothing and making her braid dance like a snake down her back. This was nature showing it was all-powerful, and she felt like she was a part of it.

A tingling started in her fingers like static electricity was swirling around her. Breathing in the charged air felt like it was energizing her whole body. Jennie kept her eyes closed and wiggled her fingers. She laughed when the tingling grew, and it felt like her fingers were shooting sparks. It was an amazing feeling, and it grew until her whole body was tingling.

The sudden crack of thunder startled her and had her quickly returning to the trees. Standing below the branches of one of the smaller trees, she kept staring out at the water. She couldn't remember noticing any flash of lightning before hearing the sound of thunder, and the rumbling had been so close she should have noticed the flash even with her eyes closed.

Jennie waited for several minutes, but the thunderstorm seemed to have stopped as fast as it had started. *One of those one-bolt wonders, perhaps.* She smiled at her own stupid joke and turned around to walk back up to the cottage.

The solid wall of muscle hit her forehead with a thud, and she would have fallen on her ass if a pair of strong hands hadn't caught her hips. Her hands flew up to grip his thick biceps, and looking up, she found herself drowning in Trevor's warm brown gaze.

His hands on her hips pulled her closer to his body, and she couldn't help the way she leaned into him and tilted her head back to give him full access to her mouth. Firm lips pressed against hers, and the tingling sensation she had felt before raced through her body, causing her to press her body more firmly against his and open her mouth to his exploring tongue. She met his tongue with her own, and they gently explored each other's textures and tastes. Gradually, the kiss became more passionate and frantic until they broke apart, gasping for air.

Jennie had no idea how long they had been kissing. It could have been a minute or an hour.

Their eyes locked, and Trevor's lips stretched into a huge grin. "I've been wanting to do that since I met you on the plane."

She laughed. "I would've let you if you'd tried." Nobody had ever kissed her quite like that before, so passionate and giving, making her feel like the purpose of the kiss was to get to know her and make her feel good instead of the kiss being just a step on the way to make her spread her legs.

He chuckled. "It's a shame I didn't then. What are you doing outside in this weather? I was sure you'd be inside with your friends, but I decided to walk past, anyway."

Trevor had been looking for her. That was why he was there. Jennie felt a surge of happiness. "I needed some air. It's great to witness the power of nature, sobering yet amazing."

He nodded and smiled. "Yeah. I don't mind the changing weather around here. It makes life interesting."

He leaned down toward her again, and she stood on her toes to meet him halfway. He slanted his lips over hers and thrust his tongue into her mouth. Their tongues played, and the kiss quickly became fiery and frantic. His hands were on her ass, lifting her slightly and pressing her firmly against his hips, where she could feel the hard length of him pressing against her mound. He groaned, and she became aware that she was grinding her hips against him. If he asked her to have sex with him right then, she would say yes. Her body was so ready for him she felt like her pussy was going to catch fire.

Trevor slowly eased his grip on her ass and ended their kiss. He looked at her with a pained expression. "I'd like nothing more than to continue what we've started, but I've promised to help a friend, and I have to go. Can I call on you tomorrow?"

Jennie could only nod. Her brain wasn't able to come up with any suitable words.

He smiled. "See you tomorrow then."

Then, he turned around and disappeared in between the trees.

Jennie's body was on fire, and she hurried up the path to the cottage. After unlocking the door to her bedroom, she walked inside and locked it behind her. She leaned against the door and closed her eyes. It was probably for the best that Trevor had stopped them before they went any further. Letting him fuck her on the forest floor wasn't exactly how she had envisioned their first time together, and she had already fantasized about that several times.

She was wet and aching with need, and judging by the rock-hard feel of his cock, he probably wasn't any better off at the moment. The first touch of his lips against hers had started a fire burning inside her unlike anything she had experienced before, and Jennie had been powerless to pull away. Not that she had wanted to.

She sucked in a deep breath to try to calm down. When she opened her eyes, they landed on her laptop, and the next scene of her story started unfolding in her mind. Jennie quickly turned on her laptop and sat down to document the events playing out inside her head.

***

Trevor hurried away from Jennie before he could change his mind. Every fiber in his body was urging him to go back to her and finish what they had started, but taking her roughly against a tree just wasn't right. She deserved to be worshipped like a queen and pleasured to the edge of sanity in a soft bed, not fucked under a tree where anyone could catch them. That kind of humiliation was unacceptable, and even his almost irresistible urge to watch her come on his cock wasn't enough to risk it.

He adjusted his hard-as-steel member, but it was still pressing uncomfortably against the zipper of his pants. The feel of Jennie's soft lips against his had filled his cock in two seconds flat, and the way she had moved her pelvis to rub against him had almost been his undoing.

Trevor groaned. He hadn't lied to her. He had promised Duncan to help him repair a window at a neighbor's house. Getting there with his pants looking like a tent would be inappropriate, though, and his cock remembered Jennie with such fondness it didn't want to listen to his plea to calm down.

He was still within the trees along the edge of the sea loch. Walking in between a few younger trees densely covered in leaves, he stopped and looked down at his straining zipper. Trevor felt like a teenager for doing this, but it was the only solution he could come up with on short notice.

He flicked open the button of his pants and pulled down the zipper, his shaft springing out in all its glory. He fisted his cock and started moving his hand up and down from base to tip. Thoughts of the way Jennie's ass had felt in his hands and how she had moved against him had his balls pull up tight, and precum soon coated the swollen head of his shaft. Her soft lips had felt like heaven, and it made him think of another soft and wet place on her body he would like to get to know.

His whole body jerked when he came and pumped his seed into his leafy surroundings. Still breathing hard from the force of his climax, Trevor opened his eyes to discover he was kneeling in the dry leaves on the ground.

ooooo

Michael rounded the corner of the cottage and soon stood in front of the door to Jennie's room. She had disappeared soon after they had returned from their outing, mumbling something about writing. He was aware she was an author and had published several novels, but he found the ability to write a fictional story difficult to understand. Michael didn't read books. When he felt like reading, he usually bought a car magazine.

At least Jennie wouldn't have to write anymore when she mated him. His family was rich, and she would be well provided for. She would be expected to be hostess at times and help organize family gatherings and business meetings, but it was only a couple of times a week. They would need to upgrade her wardrobe along with setting up a regimen for beauty treatments and regular workouts with the rest of the females in his family. As his mate she would be respected but also expected to handle herself well in any social setting within and outside his family.

Michael realized he had been standing outside Jennie's door for several minutes. He pulled in a deep breath before knocking on her door.

"Coming."

A chair scraped along the floor, and he heard Jennie walking toward the door. The door opened, and Jennie looked at him with a preoccupied expression on her face.

"Are you all right?"

She suddenly smiled and shook her head as if to clear it. "Yes, just finishing off a scene. I need five minutes."

"Okay."

The door closed in his face, and Michael stood there a bit stunned. Jennie was obviously busy finishing off a section of her book, and her whole mind was focused on that. He had no previous experience with authors and hadn't realized that was how they worked.

***

Jennie finished writing down the scene that had been playing out in her head. Closing down her laptop, she took a deep breath and tried to force her shoulders down. They had slowly crept up toward her ears while she had been writing, and she had been so focused on what was happening in her story she hadn't noticed how her shoulders were starting to cramp.

Walking into the kitchen, she saw the others were already setting the table for dinner, but checking her watch, she realized it was almost eight o'clock. As often happened when she was writing, she had completely lost track of the time.

"I'm sorry I didn't help out. I didn't realize it was this late already."

Marna laughed. "We know. You were writing."

They all sat down for dinner, and the conversation flowed freely. The events from earlier that day were all but forgotten, their focus instead on the following day's adventure.

Jennie had never been kayaking before, and most of the others hadn't either. Michael was the only one who had tried it, but that was a few years ago and only for a couple of hours. It would be interesting to see how it would work out in the morning. She had a feeling she might visit the fish more than once.

Outside it had started raining and combined with the wind, it provided a constant background music to their meal. It was nice sitting inside the rustic kitchen, enjoying good food while the elements were playing outside.

They got up to go into the living room, and Jennie

offered to do the dishes. Michael wanted to help, and she ended up alone in the kitchen with him like she had that morning.

"Are you sure you don't want to sleep in my room tonight?"

Jennie's jaw dropped at Michael's question, and she turned to look at him. She had hoped he would have gotten the message already.

"Sorry, I didn't mean it like that. We can still switch rooms if it'll make you feel safer sleeping in here." Michael was studying her face like he was trying to find out what she was thinking.

She closed her mouth and smiled at him. "I feel perfectly safe in my room, Michael, but thank you for offering. That's considerate of you."

"You could stay in my room, anyway, you know. I'd make sure you had a good time." Michael's voice was soft and sincere, with no trace of the arrogance he had shown several times before.

Shit. Jennie inwardly cursed. This was exactly the kind of suggestion she didn't want from him, and when he delivered his offer so straight forward without the typical assumption that she would fall all over herself at his offer, she felt obligated to let him down nicely.

She turned to him. "Michael, I'm not looking for a relationship right now. And particularly on a trip like this, it would be unwise to start something that might not work out. It would ruin the rest of the trip for us and for all of our friends. So, I'm sorry. I can't do that."

Michael looked at her with a neutral expression on his face, making it impossible to guess what he was thinking. "We could be good together. If you were mine, I'd make sure you had everything you ever wanted."

Jennie didn't know what to say. What he was offering sounded like far more than sex. Was this some kind of marriage proposal in disguise? It couldn't be. That would be strange when they hadn't even kissed yet. Well, he had kissed her, but that peck on her lips didn't really count as a proper kiss.

She turned back to the plate she was washing. "Michael, as I said, I don't want to start anything on this trip that might not work out."

Michael didn't say anything more, and Jennie kept her eyes on the dishes she was washing. As soon as she finished them, she cleaned off the kitchen table and the counters before going to the bathroom to get ready for bed. After brushing her teeth, she went by the living room and said goodnight to the couples. Thankfully, Michael wasn't there, and she managed to get to her room without running into him.

Jennie made sure to lock her door, but she had a feeling the guys on the beach wouldn't be back to bug them. Her brief encounter with Trevor among the trees hadn't given her an opportunity to question him about the incident with the strangers, but she would make sure to do that later. She was curious as to why those guys got so scared when she told them Trevor would vouch for her and her friends.

She smiled when she thought about seeing Trevor again. Hopefully, they would share a few more of those kisses. The only problem was that it would be difficult not to let it go any further.

Jennie went to the mirror on the wall by the bed.

Her hair was a bit messy with some of her long blond strands having escaped from her braid. The dark-blue eyes looking back at her were serious at the moment, and perhaps even a bit sad.

Standing there staring at herself, she made a decision. If the opportunity to have sex with Trevor presented itself, she would take it. A fling would be good for her, even if it was only going to be a one-night stand.

CHAPTER 9

Golden eyes were staring into hers, but she wasn't scared. It was comforting looking into those eyes. She felt safe and protected. Nothing would harm her as long as those eyes were watching over her.

Something soft and warm stroked her cheek, like it was made of fur. She wasn't able to turn her head to see whose fur it was. It was a man's, but she couldn't tell who. She reached out with her hand to grab whoever it was, but then the dream melted away.

Jennie woke up and stared up at the ceiling of her room. What an odd dream. Golden eyes, animal eyes, but at the same time they seemed human. And fur that she was sure belonged to a man. Chuckling, she sat up. She must be going insane.

It was early, but she felt completely rested. Knowing her friends, she had a while before they got up. She dressed in a short pink skirt and a white T-shirt before opening her door. It was sunny with blue skies again, but it had been raining most of the night.

She walked barefoot around the corner, even though it was still wet on the ground, and entered the main part of the house. Jennie went to the bathroom and brushed her teeth before walking into the kitchen to make herself a cup of coffee. The living room was located between the kitchen and the three bedrooms, so the sounds she made wouldn't disturb her friends.

Grabbing the coffee and a few paper towels, she went back outside. It was the perfect time to get some writing done. Writing in the morning when everything was quiet was her favorite time. She wiped off the picnic table and picked up her laptop from her room. The table would be in the shade of the trees for at least another hour.

The story unfolded as she wrote, and her two main characters were getting hot and heavy. The details of what they were doing flew from her fingertips.

"That's the perfect way to spend a beautiful morning."

Jennie jumped and let out a little squeak.

"I'm sorry, I didn't mean to scare you again." Trevor's dark voice seemed even deeper than usual.

She turned around and looked up at him. His brown eyes were darker than she remembered and looked hungry.

Jennie blushed. "Were you reading over my shoulder?"

Trevor lowered his gaze to his feet. "It wasn't my intention, but I caught a couple of words and couldn't help reading on. They seemed to be having a lot of fun." He met her eyes again, and there was no mistaking the desire in them.

It was her turn to look away. "Yes, well, somebody

sure needs to." She inwardly groaned. Why did she say that? It sounded bitter and needy.

"So, you haven't had a lot of fun lately, then?"

They both knew exactly what he was asking, and she was momentarily speechless. How was she going to answer that without sounding like a prude? Jennie decided to tell him the truth.

"Not since my divorce two years ago. I haven't really found anyone I wanted to have fun with, until perhaps last night."

"So, you want to have some fun with me while you're here?"

Jennie's eyes snapped to his in shock at his directness, but as they stared into each other's eyes, she realized he was being sincere.

"You're offering to be my vacation sex toy?"

A huge grin broke out on Trevor's face, and he chuckled. "I guess you could put it that way." Then, his eyes turned serious. "You're beautiful, Jennie, and I haven't had a lover in some time. I'd like to make you scream."

Her jaw dropped. That was blunt. And scream? Really? "Um, okay. Not here, though, and I don't think I have time before tonight. We're going kayaking today, and the others will be getting up soon."

"We can go to my house. When do you want me to pick you up tonight?" The way he was studying her face like he was trying to store a detailed image of her in his memory felt like a compliment, and it made her stomach flutter with anticipation.

"Is ten thirty okay? And do you mind if we meet down by the water?" She pointed through the trees toward where they met the day before.

"You don't want your friends to know you're getting it on with one of the locals?" His eyes shone with amusement.

Jennie snorted and gave him a small smile. "I guess."

"That's fine. Ten thirty by the water." Trevor gave her a small nod before walking away.

She stared at his back as he disappeared down the path through the trees. Her whole body tingled with excitement. She had just agreed to have sex with Trevor, a beautiful bear of a man. It was so unlike her to do something like that, but if she was going to be honest with herself, it was about time. She deserved to have some fun, and she couldn't think of anyone she would rather have sex with than Trevor.

The sound of footsteps came from around the corner of the cottage, and Jennie quickly saved her work and shut down her laptop.

"Good morning."

She turned her head to see Michael standing a couple of yards away, smiling at her. It was a bit strange seeing him smile like that after what had happened last night. And particularly after she had just agreed to have sex with someone else after saying no to him.

"Good morning, Michael."

He was holding a steaming cup in his hand. "Would you like some coffee?"

Jennie gave him what she hoped was a polite smile. He was being nice to her, so she was going to be nice back. Hopefully, that didn't give him the impression that she had changed her mind about him. "Okay, thank you. The other one got cold before I managed to finish it."

"What are you writing?"

"A paranormal romance novel. I usually get inspired to write when I go away on vacation." She took a sip of the coffee and noticed the mug was a thick ceramic variety with the outline of a wolf scratched into the material.

"So, getting to know new people inspires you?"

"Quite often, yes."

She looked up to see his smile change into a self-satisfied grin and realized he thought she was referring to him. Barely stopping herself from shuddering at the thought, she blurted the first thing that came to mind to try to stop him from thinking she was attracted to him. How could he even think that after last night?

"It's usually someone who surprises me or does something extraordinary." Hopefully, Michael would understand that didn't include him.

His grin quickly turned into a scowl. "Like that bastard at the airport. He did that just to impress you. If we hadn't been there waiting for you, he'd have invited you for sex to exploit your gratitude."

Jennie felt her anger rising and narrowed her eyes at him. "So, that's what you would've done." Trevor had invited her to have sex with him, and she was more than willing to accept his invitation because it was what she wanted too. It had nothing to do with being exploited. "Trevor—"

Michael didn't allow her to continue. "Trevor." He almost spat the word. "Did he ask for your phone number?"

Oh, this was just too ridiculous. "No, but he did invite me for sex, and I accepted."

Michael gaped at her, and she used the opportunity to walk away from him.

Jennie entered the cottage to see her friends preparing breakfast.

"Good morning. Did you sleep well out there?" Ann was smiling at her.

"Yes, like a baby. And you?"

"Like a rock."

"Exhaustion from sex will do that to you." James had moved up behind Ann to nibble on her ear suggestively.

Laughing and squealing, Ann jumped away from him. "James, we're not alone."

"Too bad." He winked at Ann before returning to the bacon he was frying.

Ann shook her head with a huge grin on her face. "Please excuse him. It must be something in the air around here. Not that I'm complaining."

Jennie smiled. It was good to see her friends' marriages were thriving.

***

It took a few seconds for Michael to realize that Jennie had only said that because she was angry with him. She hadn't actually agreed to have sex with Trevor.

He had fucked up again by showing he didn't trust her, but it had really pissed him off when he realized the asshole at the airport was still occupying her mind. Because it had to be Trevor she was referring to when she said she was inspired by someone doing something extraordinary. Who else could it be?

Michael had to get a grip, though. Until he had secured her affection and she was mated to him, he had to be on his best behavior, even if that meant ignoring his anger and frustration at her stubbornness and denial.

Pursuing Jennie had turned out to be far more difficult than he had anticipated. He had been confident that she would be flattered by his attention and fall for him easily. Women usually did. Michael knew he was good-looking and with his family's money as an added bonus, he didn't have much experience with rejection. The resistance Jennie was showing was starting to get annoying. It was all about playing hard to get, of course, but she was taking it a bit too far.

He sighed. If it wasn't for her amazing body, he would have reconsidered his idea to mate her. He was running out of time, though, and she would be a good match for him when he managed to turn her no into a yes.

∞∞∞

They arrived at the small marina a few minutes before eleven o'clock. Six kayaks were already laid out on the small beach next to the marina, and there was a pile of wetsuits, paddles, and life vests on the grass nearby.

"You must be the guys and girls wanting to kayak." They turned to see a big man walking toward them, wearing nothing but swimming shorts. "I'm Duncan, and I'll give you some pointers before you head out."

They all shook his hand and introduced themselves, and he repeated their names like it was his way of memorizing them. The way he said her name, though, it seemed like he already knew whom she was, but it must have been her imagination. She had never met this guy before.

Duncan was definite eye candy, and if she hadn't already been hung up on Trevor, she might have liked to get to know him better. He was about Trevor's height with short curly brown hair and almost black eyes, and he appeared to be one of those people who were perpetually amused. His body was seriously built. He had thick shoulders and arms with rippling muscles, a massive chest, and abs that would make a body builder cry with envy.

Jennie listened as he started describing the various parts of the kayak and how they worked. She had always just thought of a kayak as a covered canoe, but apparently that was far from correct.

There was a rudder at the back that you could use to steer by moving two pedals inside the kayak with your feet. The paddle had a blade at each end, and you were supposed to continuously move the paddle from side to side to go straight forward.

Duncan grabbed one of the paddles and pulled one of the kayaks down to the water. He straddled the boat and sat down on the back edge of the cockpit before moving his feet carefully into the boat. Then, he gripped the sides of the cockpit and slid down into the seat. It looked so easy, but she had a feeling she might take a few dives before she managed to get into that thing.

The big man proceeded to show them how to paddle efficiently using their back muscles more than their arms, and how to twist the paddle to be able to use the blade correctly on both sides.

Duncan beached the kayak and got out. “Get in and just paddle around here for a little while. I’ll give you some help to get you going.”

They each found a wetsuit and life vest. Jennie stripped down to the bikini she wore underneath her clothes before putting on her wet suit. It was a tight fit with her slightly generous frame, but she managed to wriggle into it. When she checked how the others were doing, she caught Michael staring at her, and the heat in his eyes had her turning away. It felt uncomfortable with his eyes on her like that.

Jennie put on her life vest and grabbed a paddle before heading over to one of the kayaks. James was already on the water looking like he had done this a million times before, and Carlos and Michael were both trying to get in without ending up in the water. Ann and Marna were putting on their life vests.

Jennie pulled the kayak she had chosen down to the water and positioned it with the tail end still on the beach like Duncan had shown them. She straddled it and sat down on the back edge of the cockpit. But each time she tried to pull a foot out of the water, the kayak started tilting to one side.

“Here, let me help you.” Duncan waded into the water and grabbed onto the front of her kayak. “If you need to grab the sides of the kayak for balance, make sure to push down with the same force on each side, otherwise you’ll tip over.”

She sighed. “That’s easier said than done.”

He chuckled. “Yes, it usually takes a bit of practice. You should loosen up your hips as well. Try keeping your torso upright at all times and let your hips move with the kayak.”

Jennie carefully adjusted to find her balance before slowly lifting her feet into the kayak. She made sure to balance her weight evenly on her arms while sliding down into the seat.

"I did it!" She gave Duncan a huge grin.

"Great job." He returned her grin, and then added in a whisper, "Trevor's really into you. You should give him a chance."

She quickly glanced around at the others, but they were all well out of earshot.

"I don't really know him, but I've said yes to…" She trailed off and blushed. "Um, spend some time with him." Jennie had almost blurted out that she was going to have sex with Trevor to a complete stranger. Duncan felt safe, though, and he was obviously a friend of Trevor. A warm feeling suffused her chest when she realized Trevor had mentioned her, and in a very positive way, too, by the sound of it.

"Good." His eyes were practically overflowing with amusement. "Now start paddling, and keep those hips moving," he added in a normal voice.

Her face was burning when she started paddling away from Duncan. Jennie paddled slowly to make sure she twisted the paddle correctly. Putting her feet on the pedals, she tried to steer the kayak to the right to end up circling back toward the beach.

It took all her concentration to focus on everything at once, and she forgot to look where she was going before it was too late. There was suddenly another kayak in front of her, and she caught an angry stare from Michael, before she crashed into the side of his kayak.

Jennie felt her boat tilt to the side and was suddenly

hanging upside down underneath the kayak, immersed in water. She froze. This wasn't something she had been prepared for. Capsizing and falling out was one thing but hanging upside down was something totally different.

Think, Jennie, think. She was close to the beach, so it wasn't far to swim. Putting her hands on the side of the cockpit, she pushed herself down and out of the kayak. As she was rising toward the surface, she felt a pair of strong hands grab her sides beneath her arms and propel her upward.

They broke the surface, and she sucked in a big lungful of air. When she opened her eyes, she stared directly into Duncan's worried black ones.

"Are you all right?"

"Yes." She nodded. "I'm fine. Thank you."

"Good. Can you swim?"

"Yes."

"Swim to the beach. I'll bring your kayak."

Jennie swam toward the beach. All the others were still in their kayaks, but they were headed toward the beach as well.

As she walked onto the beach, Michael beached his kayak right next to her.

She gave him an apologetic smile. "I'm sorry, I didn't mean to run into you like that. I was so busy trying to do everything correctly that I didn't look where I was going."

Michael shrugged and smiled at her. "It's fine. Next time you should pay better attention, though, or you might end up hurting yourself."

"What the hell are you playing at?" The booming voice from behind them startled Jennie. "You put yourself directly in her path on purpose." Duncan walked right up to Michael, their chests only separated by a couple of inches.

Michael's eyes narrowed in disdain. "That's bullshit. Why the fuck would I do that?"

Duncan looked furious. His lips were pulled back to reveal his teeth, and his canines seemed a little longer than normal. Jennie couldn't remember noticing that before.

"I saw you keeping an eye on her, and how you steered your kayak to end up directly in front of her. Why?"

Michael suddenly backed a couple of steps away from Duncan and put his hands up as if in defeat. "I'm so sorry, Jennie." He looked apologetic when he turned his attention to her. "Perhaps it looked like I put myself in your path on purpose, but it really wasn't intentional. Are you okay?" The concerned expression on his face looked genuine.

Jennie didn't know what to believe, but she didn't like violence. The last thing she wanted was for the two men to start fighting.

"It's okay. I'm fine." She looked at Duncan and Michael in turn. "I'll make sure to keep an eye on where I'm going next time."

"Are you all right?" Marna shouted as she came running up to them.

Jennie turned and saw the concern in her friend's eyes. Ann was following closely behind Marna.

She smiled at them. "I'm fine, just a bit wet that's all. The good thing is that I now know what to do if I capsize."

Duncan laughed. "You're not squeamish, are you.

That's a good quality."

They talked for a while and asked Duncan some questions before deciding it was time to take a little trip exploring the area.

"Stay close to the shore at all times in case anything happens, and take care of each other." Duncan threw Michael a stern look. "You can put your food and clothes inside the waterproof compartments in your kayaks. I'll be here at four to retrieve the equipment."

"Thank you, Duncan." Jennie smiled at him as he turned to go.

He stopped. "You're not scared at all?"

She shook her head. "No, I'm not scared of the water. If I tip over again, I'll just get out and pull the kayak to shore to get in again."

He chuckled. "That's the spirit. See you at four."

"See you."

Jennie walked down to her kayak and put her packed lunch and her clothes in the front compartment. She managed to get into the kayak on the second try and paddled a few strokes away from the beach to wait for Marna and Ann. This was more fun than she had thought it would be. Even tipping over had been kind of fun, at least in hindsight.

CHAPTER 10

Duncan strode into the kitchen, where Trevor was just finishing his lunch.

"I made enough omelet for you as well." Trevor nodded toward the stove. "How did it go? Was Jennie there?"

Duncan chuckled. "Yeah, and she's got balls that one."

Trevor grinned. "I fucking hope not. I'd like to find something else down there."

"When do you plan to find out?" Duncan's eyes were filled with amusement. "I got the impression it might be soon."

Trevor was surprised. "What? Did she say something?"

"She said she'd agreed to spend time with you. I got the feeling she meant that in an intimate sense."

Trevor didn't want to give too much away. He felt protective of Jennie, and admitting to propositioning her for sex like she was some kind of loose woman didn't sit well with him. Even if this was Duncan he was talking to, one of his best friends.

"We'll see what happens. I'm going to pick her up tonight."

"As in bring her here? Do you want me out of the house tonight?" Duncan put his overflowing plate down on the table across from Trevor and sat down. "There's a lass over in Fort William who doesn't usually turn me away."

"If you don't mind." Trevor studied his friend. "Business or pleasure?"

Duncan laughed. "I'm not interested in getting serious with anyone. Way too much hassle. I'm all about the pleasure and the lass knows that's all she'll ever get from me."

Trevor smiled. He knew the feeling well. Settling down with someone had never tempted him until these last few days. But he couldn't settle down with Jennie. He'd give her pleasure, though, as much as she could take.

"At least one of the guys traveling with her is a shifter, and I don't like him."

Trevor's eyes snapped to Duncan's to see them narrowed in a frown.

"What do you mean?"

"He stared at Jennie while she was changing into her wetsuit, clearly attracted to her. But later, as they were testing the kayaks on the water, he put himself intentionally in her path. She ran her kayak into his and tipped over."

"Is she all right?" Trevor was on his feet, ready to go to her.

"Jennie's fine. As I said, she's got balls. She got out

of the kayak on her own, and she's a good swimmer. It didn't take long before she was ready to go back out there. I just don't understand what the asshole was hoping to achieve by sinking her, or if it was payback for something."

Trevor felt his canines elongating. "They're still out there?"

Duncan looked at him. "Calm down. I confronted him and he backed down quickly. I think he knows I'd hurt him if something happened to her."

Trevor swore. "I'd hang him up by his balls, and that would just be for starters."

Duncan laughed. "I believe you."

Trevor sighed and tried to relax, but he didn't like Jennie staying in the same house as a single male shifter. And to make matters worse, the male was apparently attracted to her. "I sniffed around Miller's cottage last night, and there was something odd about all the males' scent. It wasn't a scent I recognized. Were you able to determine what kind of shifters they are?"

"I think they're some kind of cat, but not one I've come across before. Why don't you come with me at four to pick up the kayaks? Might be good for you to meet your rival."

Trevor growled. "He'd better not be. I'd kill him."

Duncan's eyes widened in surprise. "Are you positive Jennie's not your mate?"

"She can't be. Leave it." Trevor couldn't allow that. "I'll go with you at four."

Trevor left the kitchen and went up to his bedroom. He changed the sheets and cleaned up to make sure it was spotless. Then, he cleaned his bathroom and put in fresh towels. Looking around to make sure he hadn't overlooked anything, he considered getting some candles or fresh flowers.

Then he groaned. Jennie was going to be his lover for a few nights. This wasn't their wedding night or anything. What was wrong with him? He had never been the romantic type before. Why did he feel the urge to make this night special for her?

ooooo

They were paddling south along the coast. There was hardly any wind, so they all soon handled their kayaks with ease. Jennie was surprised at how fast they were going, even though they didn't have any experience. They were moving through the water at a much higher speed than she had ever had while paddling a canoe. Looking at the shore, she felt a bit like she was flying low over the water. It was exhilarating.

Jennie, Ann, and Marna were gliding along beside each other, although beside was perhaps a bit inaccurate. There were quite a few yards between each kayak to avoid a conflict between their paddles.

"This is great. I should've tried this earlier," Jennie shouted to her friends.

"Yes, I had no idea it was possible for a normal person like me to handle a kayak. It's not actually that difficult." When Jennie looked over at her, Marna had a huge grin on her face.

They paddled for about an hour before deciding to take a break on a small beach.

Sitting on their towels, they ate their packed

lunches and talked. Not many restaurants could rival a view and atmosphere like this.

They had all gotten out of their wetsuits and were only wearing their swimsuits. Jennie's bikini was fairly revealing but not too skimpy. But the way Michael was staring at her generous breasts whenever he thought she didn't notice made her want to cover up.

Jennie was always a bit surprised whenever a man made it known to her that he appreciated the way she looked. She had never been skinny and didn't expect men to get turned on by her body. Not that she considered herself overweight. Walking and hiking was something she really enjoyed, and she went for a long walk almost every day. She normally managed a visit to the gym once or twice a week as well, so even though she had meat on her bones, she was fit and healthy.

Michael's unwelcome interest only made her uncomfortable, though, but she didn't really want to call him out on his ogling and ruin the great day they were having.

After a while she excused herself to find a place to pee and walked down to a group of trees at one end of the beach. There were sheep in the field up from the beach, and Jennie could hear them bleating while she did her business behind some bushes.

***

Michael got up when he saw Jennie emerge from the trees and walk down toward the water. He would have liked to talk to her without having the others watching them, but that wasn't really an option at the moment.

She had been clear last night about not getting into anything with him on this trip. It was natural for her to be shy about showing her friends what was going on between them, at least until it was more settled. But he was running out of time to find a mate, and he was sure that if Jennie just spent one night with him, she would be his.

Nobody had ever complained about his skills in bed. His dad had always gone on about how it was a woman's job to take care of the man in bed, but Michael had always felt it should be the other way around. A man should provide for his woman financially as well as physically. Not to mention that watching a woman's face when she climaxed and feeling her channel tighten around his shaft turned him on like nothing else could.

Michael let his eyes take in Jennie's rounded curves as she was bending down to wash her hands in the sea. He had no problem imagining her standing like that with him behind her, pounding into her tight, wet channel. His cock twitching at the thought made him quickly think about something else. Walking up to her with a hard-on was not going to support his case, even though it would show her he had a lot to offer in that department.

She rose and turned to look at him, and he gave her his most genuine smile. If she just understood how much he had to give her, he was sure she would happily accept to be his mate.

"Jennie, I would like to talk to you about what I said last night."

She flinched but he pressed on undeterred. It would be a mistake to let her speak and give her a chance to refuse him, before he had said what he wanted to say.

"I heard what you said about not wanting to start

anything on this trip, but I don't mind being discreet if you don't want anyone else to know about us yet. I've got a lot to offer you, Jennie. If you'd only give me a chance to prove it to you, you'd find that I'm a great lover."

"Michael, I—"

He kept going, not giving her a chance to continue.

"And you'd be well provided for. I'm rich and I'd make sure you had everything you ever wanted. You don't have to work another day in your life. We can spend time traveling, and when the time is right, we can have children. Kids are highly valued in my family, and we'll have the financial means to let them choose whatever they want to do with their lives."

***

"Michael!" Jennie was horrified by his intense speech. She had hoped he had gotten the message last night, but he obviously hadn't. "I'm not in love with you. If you somehow got that impression, I'm sorry. You should find someone who cares about you in that way."

He almost looked a bit sad for a moment, but then his expression changed into one of determination.

"I accept that you're not in love with me, but what I can give you will compensate for that. Feelings can't be relied on, anyway, and usually just complicate things."

Jennie didn't know what to say. Did he actually expect her to agree to marry him like it was some kind of business transaction? And he hadn't said anything about being in love with her either. Why would he want to marry her if he didn't love her?

"What's in it for you? I don't understand why you'd

want to marry me if you're not in love with me."

Michael frowned like he didn't really understand the question. "You're beautiful and I'm attracted to you. I'm looking forward to having you in my bed every night, and you'll enjoy it. It's a man's job to provide for his woman, financially as well as in the bedroom."

Jennie was speechless. This was beyond awkward and by far the weirdest offer she had ever gotten.

Michael suddenly smiled at her. "I understand it's a bit much to take in. I'll leave you to think about it, and we can talk more later." And before she could find her voice, he turned around and walked back along the beach toward the others.

"Shit, shit, shit." Jennie cursed in a low voice. This was so fucked up. How could he think she would agree to marry him? Particularly when he realized she wasn't in love with him. But that didn't even seem to matter. Perhaps he even preferred her not to have feelings for him. Less complicated, as he put it.

She was utterly shocked, though. This was so far away from her way of thinking she wasn't sure how to even explain it to Michael that this wasn't something she would ever consider. Jennie would rather be alone for the rest of her life than willingly subject herself to an arrangement like that. But she knew there were plenty of women who would jump at an opportunity like that. She just wasn't one of them.

Jennie slowly made her way along the beach to the others, and after a little while, they packed up. It was time to head back to Fearolc to return the kayaks.

CHAPTER 11

Jennie felt like a pro paddling toward the beach. She was really starting to get the hang of this, and it was fun. It was a shame it was over, and they were going to give back the equipment. Perhaps they could rent the kayaks again another day.

Michael's offer had bothered her for a while, but paddling alongside Ann and Marna on the way back, exchanging friendly banter, had made her realize there was a simple solution. She would wait until he brought it up again and then tell him no. And if he didn't want to accept her refusal, she would tell Ann and Marna about his offer. They would be just as horrified as she was and would help her convince him that no was her final answer.

As she approached the beach, two men rounded the corner of the large equipment shed and headed toward the beach. One of them was Duncan and the other was…Jennie's heart skipped a beat when she saw him. Trevor. He was wearing swimming shorts like

Duncan, but unlike Duncan who was still bare-chested, Trevor was sporting a white T-shirt. But instead of hiding his sexiness, it somehow made him look even more mouthwatering. The T-shirt did nothing to hide his thick shoulders and prominent pecs, and his biceps, which were partially covered, looked like they were giving the material a challenge.

Their eyes met, and Jennie couldn't help the happy grin that spread across her face. Trevor's smile reflected hers, and she lost all focus. Her paddle hit the water flat, and before she realized what was happening, she was tilting to the side.

She silently swore as she ended up upside down in the water again. Way to make a good impression. He would think she was an incompetent moron.

Jennie pushed herself out of the kayak, but before she could rise to the surface, she felt two strong arms wrap around her, and she was pressed against a massive chest. There was no doubt in her mind it was Trevor holding her. He brought them quickly to the surface.

Staring into her eyes, he studied her with concern etched on his face. "Are you okay?"

She smiled. "Of course—it's just water. I'm a bit embarrassed, though. I thought I'd mastered the technique."

Trevor laughed. "Accidents do happen, even to masters." Then he lowered his arms, grabbed her ass cheeks with his hands, and gave them a squeeze before letting her go.

Trevor turned her kayak the right way up and pulled it as they swam to the beach. The others were already there, taking off their wetsuits.

"Hi, Jennie." Duncan's amusement was evident as he let his gaze glide from her to Trevor and back.

"Hi, Duncan. Guess I still need some practice."

His expression turned serious. "Have you capsized many times today?"

She laughed. "No, not since this morning. Don't look so concerned. I know how to get out of the damn thing under water. I would've been fine."

Duncan chuckled. "Yes, sorry. I realize you can take care of yourself. I didn't mean to imply otherwise."

Jennie just smiled. "It's okay." She looked at Trevor. "Thank you for rescuing me."

"But you would've been fine without me." Trevor smiled. "I get it, but you know, damsel in distress and all that."

She grinned. "You couldn't help yourself, could you?"

Trevor shook his head. "Nope. Goes against every fiber of my being not to help a beautiful lady in need."

Jennie glanced over at her friends. They were just about ready to leave.

She stretched her hand up behind her back to grab the string tied to the zipper on the back of the wetsuit and pulled it down. Starting to wriggle out of the thing, she looked up at Trevor. He was looking totally mouthwatering with his wet white T-shirt molded to his torso, showing off each perfect muscle. Duncan had already gone to gather all the equipment they had used.

"My friends are waiting for me. I have to go."

Trevor's eyes followed her movements as she peeled the wetsuit down to her thighs to reveal her pink and turquoise bikini. His gaze darkened as he studied her breasts before moving his gaze down her stomach to the apex of her thighs.

His eyes suddenly snapped back up to hers, and he whispered too low for the others to hear. "I guess I'll see you tonight then."

She nodded, and he turned around and walked toward the kayaks her friends had left on the beach.

Jennie pulled the wetsuit off her legs and put it with the other equipment. Then, she went down to the kayak she had used and removed her things from the front compartment. They were all still dry. She put on her flip-flops and wrapped her towel around her waist before walking up to her friends, who were waiting for her.

They were all looking like they were about to burst out laughing, except for Michael, who was looking away with a neutral expression on his face.

"What?" She frowned at them.

"Later," Ann and Marna said at the same time.

They waved and yelled thank you and goodbye to Duncan and Trevor before walking off down the road toward their cottage.

"Now tell me what's so hilarious." Jennie looked at Ann and Marna. They were walking a little behind the men.

"That was the guy from the airport, wasn't it?" Ann was practically jumping from excitement. "And he likes you."

"You should've seen his face when you tipped over," Marna gushed. "And I don't think I've ever seen anyone move that fast."

Jennie shrugged. "It's all about the damsel in

distress notion. I guess some men are naturally protective of women."

Ann laughed. "Oh, I don't think it's got anything to do with women in general. I think this guy is all about you."

"Perhaps it's just what the men around here are like. Duncan saved me the first time."

Marna looked unconvinced. "Maybe. I still think the blond-haired guy likes you."

When they got back to the cottage, they took turns taking a shower. It felt good cleaning off the salt, sand, and sunscreen.

They relaxed outside for a while with beers before making dinner and sitting down at the picnic table outside to eat. They discussed the hiking trails in the area again and decided on a trail up into the hills for the following day.

Michael had been silent throughout dinner, but as they were clearing off the table and bringing all the dishes to the kitchen to clean, he smiled and joked.

Jennie offered to do the dishes, and Michael wanted to help. Then he turned to the others.

"Why don't you guys go for an evening stroll while we clean up here?"

The two couples decided to go for a walk, and she was left in the kitchen alone with Michael. He was all smiles and politeness, and she tried to relax as they chatted about everything and nothing while they cleaned up. Perhaps he had finally realized it was stupid pursuing her and was just trying to be her friend instead. That would be great.

"I liked kayaking today." Jennie smiled at him. "They were so fast once you figured out the paddling technique, much faster than paddling a canoe. Maybe we can rent them another day before we leave."

"Was it the kayaks you liked or the guys renting them out?" Michael suddenly looked angry.

Jennie couldn't believe it. This guy was such an asshole. "You know. That's none of your concern. I can feel and act however I please, and if that annoys you, then stay the hell away from me." She'd had enough of his crap. Jennie rinsed off the last pot and put it on the rack before turning around to go.

"Did you tip your kayak on purpose to get Trevor's attention? You knew he was going to be there, didn't you? Did you tell Duncan to bring Trevor along this afternoon so you could put on a show for him?"

Jennie felt her anger explode and turned back to him. "You're an asshole, do you know that? If I was into a man, do you really think I'd purposely act like a moron in front of him? That's not the impression I like to make. Stay away from me, Michael. You're giving me whiplash with your mood swings."

She walked out the door and went to her room around the corner. Sitting down on her bed, she tried to calm down. What was wrong with this guy? If he actually wanted her to marry him, he had a really funny way of trying to persuade her. She could understand if he got jealous when seeing her interact with guys like Trevor and Duncan, but accusing her of being an idiot? There was no excuse for that.

Jennie went to the desk and opened her laptop. Maybe she could write for a while. It was still almost two hours until she was going to meet Trevor. She smiled, thinking about it, and her body started tingling all over in anticipation. Well, there was no doubt she had a crush on him. No serious feelings of course, but Jennie was really looking forward to seeing him again.

She hadn't expected to see him on the beach. That had been a small shock to her system but in a pleasant way. Trevor had seemed happy to see her as well. Jennie thought about how his big hands had felt squeezing her ass, and heat gathered low in her belly in anticipation of their night together. She was looking forward to gripping those big firm biceps and letting her hands glide over his well-developed pecs and ripped abs. The white T-shirt he had been wearing had stuck to his body when he emerged from the water, and that image was etched into her retinas, making her squirm in her chair. Well, she had better focus on something else or she would jump Trevor without any preamble when she saw him later.

Jennie read through the last few pages of the novel she was writing to get into the story again. It didn't take long before the words started flowing, and she was lost in her invented world. She kept an eye on the time, though, to make sure she wasn't going to be late for her date. Or date might be pushing it—it was more like a sex appointment.

ꝏꝏꝏ

Michael silently swore when Jennie stormed out the door. He had been doing so well talking lightly and making her laugh, but the sight of her undressing in front of that gorilla had been eating at him. And then he had fucked up. Again.

Jennie obviously liked the asshole, but Michael didn't actually think she had anything to do with him turning up this afternoon. Both Duncan and Trevor were wolves, and it wasn't a stretch to assume they exchanged information about single females in the area. Michael would have to be more on guard in the future, to prevent Jennie from getting to know the asshole better. As far as he knew she wasn't one to jump into bed with someone after knowing them for a couple of days, but he wasn't going to leave that to chance.

Michael would give her some time to calm down before apologizing. He didn't want to make it even worse by approaching her too soon.

∞∞∞

At ten o'clock Jennie saved her work and shut down her laptop. She went into the house and did what she usually did to prepare for bed. Then, she went into the living room. Both the couples were there, but Michael was nowhere to be seen. Thank goodness for small favors.

"I think I'll call it an early night. I hope you don't mind."

They smiled at her, and Ann spoke for all of them. "No, I think we might head off to bed quite soon as well. She threw her husband a coy smile, and he nodded with a wicked grin on his face.

Jennie smiled. "All right, sleep tight. See you in the morning."

As she was exiting the cottage, she almost crashed into Michael. He stopped and looked like he was going to say something, but she quickly cut him off.

"I'm going to bed. Good night."

She quickly stepped around him and went to her room. She waited inside the door for a minute, but she didn't hear any footsteps outside.

Jennie decided to put on one of her summer dresses. She picked a short white dress with large blue flowers on the skirt. It wasn't tight, but it showed off her breasts nicely. Then, she brushed out her long blond hair and braided it to fall forward over one shoulder.

After exiting her room, she locked the door and hid the key underneath one of the rocks in the flower bed next to the door. Everyone would think she had gone to bed, so nobody would be looking for a key outside.

She darted quickly and quietly down the path through the trees and soon emerged on the shore of the sea loch.

***

Trevor stood within the trees a little to the side of the path when Jennie suddenly burst out of the trees. The sight of her bouncing breasts in the little white and blue dress she wore rendered him speechless. She was stunning, and he felt his cock start swelling. That snapped him out of his frozen state. Sporting a big hard-on like some teenager from watching her breasts bounce was not the way to impress this beautiful woman.

He focused on her face and stepped out of the trees. "You look beautiful, Jennie."

She beamed at him, and he couldn't help grinning back like an idiot. "Thank you. So do you." Her eyes wandered from his face slowly down his body, and he tried to focus on breathing calmly to avoid his cock from responding to her checking him out. Quickly stepping up to her, he grabbed her hand and gave it a little tug.

"Come, let's go. If I start kissing you here, we might never get any further tonight. I want to have you in my bed and not against a tree. I'm sure that would be fun, too, but not for our first time."

Jennie fell into step beside him. "Okay." Her voice sounded a little breathless. "So, this is not just for tonight then?"

He glanced at her. "I hope not. If that's okay with you?"

She gave him a small shy smile. "That's more than okay with me."

"Good."

He brought her through the field and to his house through the gate in the stone fence.

"Wow, is this your house?" The awe in her voice had him chuckling.

"Yes, I live here when I'm in Scotland. Duncan takes care of it for me."

"So he lives here as well?" He could hear the reluctance in her voice.

Trevor opened the back door and let her walk inside ahead of him. "Yes, but he's not here tonight. He has a girl over in Fort William that he visits now and then."

Jennie turned to him with amusement in her eyes. "You mean you kicked him out for the night."

Trevor laughed. "Something like that. I don't want anyone else hearing us and causing you any embarrassment. I intend to make you scream, remember?"

CHAPTER 12

Jennie stared at Trevor as he slowly walked toward her like he was stalking prey. There was something predatory about him. His movements were so smooth and efficient, like he was accustomed to hunting animals using nothing but his body. As he stopped in front of her, she had to bend her neck back to be able to meet his eyes. She saw the raw hunger in them and felt her body respond.

Trevor's large hands gripped her upper arms gently, and he walked her backward. His eyes were intensely focused on hers. She felt the wall against her back stopping her progress, and he bent his head as if to kiss her. With his mouth an inch away from hers, he stopped, and she felt his knee nudging her legs apart. His thigh ended up pressed against her center, and her pussy clenched in response. She couldn't help the gasp that escaped her.

He let go of her upper arms and pressed his entire body into hers. Her breasts were mashed against his firm chest, and there was no mistaking the hard shaft pressing against her hip. It was so erotic she felt herself getting wet.

When his lips brushed hers, she jerked like an electric current had passed between them. He pulled back a little and paused, his eyes almost black with desire.

"Kiss me, Trevor. Please."

That was all it took. He moved his lips over hers, massaging them gently, and she responded in kind. Jennie gripped his thick shoulders to hold onto him, and when his tongue licked at the seam of her lips, she happily opened for him. Their tongues met and danced, licking and stroking each other, and she became aware that she was rubbing her pussy shamelessly against his thigh. She wasn't the only one moving, though. Trevor was grinding his cock into her hip.

He suddenly let go of her, and she let out a squeak when he bent down and hooked one arm behind her knees and one behind her back. He lifted her like she weighed nothing and strode down the hall and up the stairs to the second floor. She put a hand on his chest, feeling the solid muscles there moving as he held her tightly against him while he walked. In the corridor at the top of the stairs, he turned right and continued until they came to the door at the end. When they entered the room, she was amazed at the stylish yet homey feel of it.

The room was spacious and softly lit, but what caught her attention was the huge bed. Trevor walked right up to it and placed her in the middle. She tried to sit up, but before she could, he was on all fours above her looking down into her eyes.

His eyes seemed to burn with desire, and it made her whole body ignite with a blazing need. It was so powerful she moaned. Trevor kissed her lips gently before kissing down her jaw. She squirmed and squeezed her thighs together when he sucked on her earlobe before moving down to her collarbone.

He sat back on his knees, straddling her legs. "You look amazing in that dress, but I bet you look even better out of it." He took ahold of the hem and pulled the dress up, and she helped him by lifting her body off the bed. As soon as he threw the dress to the floor, he was back to kissing her collarbone. His hand stroked along her side before gripping the fabric of her bra covering one breast and pulling it down to reveal her nipple. When his mouth fastened around the hard peak, sucking on it, the glorious sensation sent a jolt of pleasure directly down to her clit. The small nub started throbbing with anticipation. Jennie moaned and squeezed her legs together to alleviate some of the need, but it only made it worse.

Trevor's other hand gripped her hip before moving to cup her pussy through her wet panties. He groaned and let go of her breast. "You're so wet for me."

Jennie reached up and put her arms around his neck before threading her fingers into his hair and massaging his scalp. "I want you, Trevor." Her voice was almost unrecognizable it was so husky.

Trevor attacked her breast, licking and sucking. He slid his fingers inside her panties and played along her slit.

Jennie was about ready to combust. "Please, Trevor." She wasn't above pleading. Her need to come was growing unbearable.

He chuckled against her breast. Then his thumb slowly slid up to her clit and started manipulating the small nub with increasing pressure.

Jennie wanted him inside her when she came, but she was so close to completion that words eluded her. It was hard to focus on anything other than what Trevor was doing to her body.

Trevor suddenly bit down gently on her nipple at the same time as he pressed down on her clit, and Jennie went flying. The orgasm pulsed through her body, radiating outward from her center, and Trevor kept massaging her clit, prolonging the powerful sensation.

When she came down, he inched a hand behind her back and opened the clasp of her bra. He pulled it off before proceeding to remove her panties.

Jennie looked at Trevor's chest, which was still covered by his T-shirt. "You have to remove your clothes as well. I want to see you naked."

"Yes, ma'am." Trevor met her eyes and grinned. "Anything you want."

He got off the bed and pulled his T-shirt over his head before popping the button of his cargo pants. Her eyes were glued to his groin as he pulled down the zipper, and she felt her eyes widen at the sight of his long thick cock. He was easily bigger than any man she had ever been with, and her pussy suddenly felt empty.

Jennie let her gaze glide slowly up Trevor's magnificent body. She had never been that focused on a man's muscles before, believing that his personality and the chemistry between them were more important. But there was no doubt that Trevor's muscular physique turned her on. Or perhaps it was the combination of their incredible chemistry and his powerful body that did it.

Still lying on her back, she bent her knees and let her thighs fall wide open to reveal her pussy. Trevor's eyes zeroed in on her down there, and he licked his lips.

"Are you going to fuck me or are you going to stand there all night?" She grinned up at him.

His eyes snapped to hers, and his jaw fell in surprise, but he quickly recovered and gave her a wicked grin. "Oh, I'm going to fuck you, but first I'm going to taste you."

It was Jennie's turn to be surprised, and she gaped at him. Faster than she would have thought possible, he leaned forward and grabbed her legs, pulling her toward him until her ass was resting on the edge of the bed. Then, he kneeled and put her legs over his shoulders, before his head came down between her thighs.

She felt his tongue lick all the way along her slit up to her clit, and then he sucked on the small bud. The powerful sensations he created had her writhing on the bed, and his hands clamped down on her thighs to hold her still.

***

Trevor couldn't believe how good she tasted. He kept licking and sucking on the small hard button between her thighs, and Jennie made small whimpering noises and thrashed her head from side to side.

He wanted to be inside her so badly it hurt. His cock was so hard if felt like a steel bar poking into his stomach, and his balls were pulled up tight.

"Please," Jennie moaned. "I want you inside me when I come."

Trevor wanted that, too, and who was he to deny her? He eased off her clit and stood. He walked over to his bedside table and opened the top drawer, then pulled out a box of condoms. Taking out one, he unwrapped it and put it on.

"Thank you for remembering that." Jennie smiled at him with desire shining in her eyes. "I didn't."

He smiled at her and walked back to the end of the bed. Not letting go of her eyes, he kneeled between her thighs and put her feet on his shoulders. Then he positioned his cock at her entrance and slid inside. Her eyes widened, and she gasped as her channel adjusted to accept him. He growled at the feel of her tight pussy encasing him perfectly, and he kept pushing slowly inside her until his hips met her thighs.

Trevor looked at where they were joined and felt his cock twitch. He leaned over her, and Jennie gripped his biceps and moaned as he started moving. Setting a steady pace, he watched her face, adjusting the angle of his strokes until she threw her head back and made keening noises.

Trevor was getting close. He reached between her legs and slid his thumb over her clit in small circles. Jennie's pussy tightened around his shaft, and he lost it. Pumping into her uncontrollably while fondling her clit, he felt himself coming. Jennie screamed his name, and her channel clamped down on him hard. His cock jerked violently as he came, and he snarled as the powerful orgasm spun through his body, making it vibrate with pleasure.

As he came down, he opened his eyes. Jennie's head was thrown back, and her hands were fisted in the sheets. She slowly opened her eyes, and their gazes met.

"Wow." She stared at him with amazement in her eyes.

He chuckled and did a mental fist pump. "Wow back."

Trevor slowly eased out of her and went to the bathroom to throw away the condom. He cleaned himself off and brought a wet towel back for Jennie.

He found her still lying on her back on his bed, looking around his room. She turned to him and smiled as he approached the bed. Trevor gently cleaned between her legs before climbing onto the bed with her. They moved around a bit to get under the covers.

Trevor pulled her firmly against his front, spooning her. Her body was soft and felt like heaven, and he couldn't think of anywhere he would rather be.

"Are you comfortable?" He spoke softly into her ear.

Jennie sighed, sounding content and happy. "Very." She wriggled her body against his. "Your body is so warm and firm. I like it."

"It's going to be even firmer if you keep wriggling like that."

She twisted her neck to look at him, and her eyes were round with surprise. "We just finished."

He grinned. "I recover quickly, and you're mine for a few more hours. I intend to use them wisely."

Jennie laughed. "Wisely. I like that."

***

She couldn't believe how lucky she was to be there with this amazing man. It was like a flying start to the rest of her life, a confidence booster for sure, and it would help her start dating again. Because as much as she liked Trevor, Jennie knew this fling was for a few days only. There was no future with him, and she would do well to remember that.

Before she could think more about that, though, she felt his hand inch between her legs and a finger slipping inside her. Jennie gasped in astonishment and pleasure and opened her legs a little to allow him access. He pumped one finger in and out of her pussy a few times before adding another digit. Focusing on the sensitive front wall of her channel, he kept moving his fingers, and she couldn't prevent her hips from moving to meet his strokes. His hard cock was pressed against her ass and lower back, and he started moving his hips to rub it against her.

"Jennie." Trevor's voice was deeper than usual and slightly breathless. "Can you reach the condoms on the nightstand? Otherwise, I'm going to come all over your back like some teenage boy."

She stretched out an arm and managed to grab the box. After pulling out a condom, she unwrapped it and handed it to him. He pulled a little away from her and put it on. Then his hand was suddenly back between her legs, but this time it wasn't his fingers that entered her. The hard, thick length of him breached her entrance, and she moaned. His fingers moved to her clit, playing with it as he pushed all the way inside her pussy, filling her completely.

He felt so good inside her. His big cock was a perfect fit, filling her to capacity and allowing glorious friction and pressure on all her sensitive areas. She had never felt so completely sated by anyone.

Jennie reached behind her and grabbed one of his ass cheeks and squeezed. His hot meaty flesh in her hand turned her on even more, and then he started moving.

Trevor used long slow strokes. His fingers were still fondling her clit, and Jennie lost the ability to focus on anything other than what he was doing to her body. Pleasure was building in her lower abdomen, and she gripped the sheets with the hand not holding onto his ass.

He started pumping into her faster, his movements a little erratic. "Shit, Jennie, you feel so good. I'm struggling for control here." His voice was gravelly and deep.

"I'm so close." She panted and felt her pussy tighten.

Trevor changed the angle of his strokes a little and slammed into her hard at the same time as he pinched her clit, and she erupted in pleasure. Trevor roared behind her as his cock started jerking hard inside her, making her pleasure even more intense. She heard herself screaming his name over and over as the orgasm rode her hard.

When she finally returned to this world, she was panting hard. Trevor's body was plastered against her back with one hand splayed over her stomach and his member still inside her.

He sighed. "I have to get rid of the condom." Then, he pulled out of her slowly and went to the bathroom.

When he came back out, Jennie climbed out of bed.

She gave him a happy smile. "I'll be right back." She went to the bathroom and cleaned up before returning to him.

Trevor was standing by the window, looking outside. He turned around when she approached, and his eyes dipped to her breasts. "I've spent far too little time appreciating those." When he met her eyes, the corners of his mouth pulled up in a mischievous grin.

She gaped at him and glanced down to see his cock jutting from between his legs. Was this guy for real? They had just had sex twice, and he was up for more? Up being the operative word.

Jennie shook her head in astonishment. "I thought going all night was the stuff of romance novels. But you can actually do that, can't you?"

He let his eyes caress her body from her head to her toes before bringing them back up to meet hers with a small smile on his face. "I guess with you, anything is possible."

CHAPTER 13

Jennie retrieved the key from underneath the rock in the flowerbed and unlocked the door to her room. It was five in the morning, and Trevor had just brought her back, kissing her one last time on the shore of the sea loch before leaving her to return to his house.

Her lady parts were pleasantly sore, and she had a perpetual grin on her face. She had taken a shower before leaving his house, so she was clean but tired. They had dozed off a couple of hours, and the rest of the time they had spent talking and fucking. It had been the most amazing night of passion in her life.

At first when Trevor asked her to have sex with him, she had thought he meant a one-night stand, and that had been okay with her. But a one-night stand was clearly not what he had meant. Well, not according to her definition of the term, anyway. If his definition was more like one whole night of continuous sex, then yes, it was a one-night stand.

Trevor didn't want just one night, though. He

wanted her every night while she was in Fearolc, which was completely fine by her. She would probably be exhausted and sore by the end of it, but it would be worth it.

Jennie locked the door before taking off her clothes and getting under the covers. After setting the alarm on her phone to 9:00 a.m., she lay back and fell asleep almost immediately.

She woke when someone knocked on her door.

"Just a minute," she yelled and swung her legs out of bed. Checking her phone, she noticed it was eight forty-five. At least she had gotten a few hours of sleep.

Jennie quickly threw on a T-shirt and shorts and opened the door. She was surprised to see Michael standing there, and when his eyes dipped to her chest, she felt the irritation and anger from the day before surging. But before she could say anything, he snapped his gaze back to hers.

"I'm sorry, Jennie. I was out of line yesterday."

Her jaw fell open, and she stared at him. That was not what she had expected him to say.

Then, he suddenly thrust a cup of coffee at her.

"Can you forgive me for being an asshole?" He actually looked like he was going to go down on his knees, begging for her forgiveness.

"Yes, okay, but any more accusations and bullshit, and I'll revoke my decision." She took the cup he was holding out to her. "Thank you for the coffee. Are the others up yet?"

He gave her a tentative smile. "Ann and James are in the kitchen making breakfast. I haven't seen Marna and Carlos yet."

"Okay, I'll be in the kitchen in a few minutes,

okay?"

Michael nodded and walked away.

Jennie closed the door and looked down at her chest. *Shit.* She had given him an eyeful by not wearing a bra. But she had thought it was Ann or Marna knocking on her door.

She turned off the alarm she had set for 9:00 a.m. and put on a sports bra underneath her T-shirt. Checking the mirror on the wall by the bed, she brushed her hair and braided it. After putting on some sunscreen, she was ready to go hiking through the hills.

Entering the kitchen, she was overwhelmed by the pleasant smell of bacon, and her stomach rumbled in response. No wonder, she had used a lot of energy last night.

Ann chuckled. "Someone's hungry. Well, take a seat. I'll just get the scones out of the oven."

"You made scones? When did you get up this morning?" Jennie was surprised. Ann usually liked to sleep in.

"Early, don't ask." Ann glanced over at James, who grinned back at his wife.

Jennie decided it was none of her business. "I can't wait to taste your scones."

Marna and Carlos entered the kitchen, and they all sat down to eat. Jennie kept remembering glimpses from her time last night with Trevor. It would have been nice to be able to tell her friends about her vacation fling with the gorgeous man, but it would be better to tell Ann and Marna what had happened later when they were back home. She didn't want them fussing over it and try to make it into more than it was. And then there was Michael. He had apologized for being an ass the day before, but after his strange proposal, she had a feeling that finding out she was fucking someone else would seriously piss him off. Michael had no claim on her, and after what happened last night, she hoped he realized that, but they were going to have to spend time together while they were in Scotland, and she didn't want to ruin everyone's vacation.

They made packed lunches and filled their water bottles. Chocolate, raisins, and peanuts were added as energy boosters, and they were ready to go. Carlos brought out the map and pointed out the first part of the route they would be taking up to the highest point of the mountain behind the village. They would be skirting Trevor's field where some of his sheep were kept.

They followed the main road for a few hundred yards until they found the track going up toward Trevor's field. When they came to the stone fence marking the boundary, the track continued to the right along the fence. Jennie kept sneaking peeks toward where she could see Trevor's house between the trees lining his lawn, but there was no sign of anyone out and about.

The track left the stone fence, and they followed it as it gradually became steeper. Tracks occasionally branched off to the left or right, but Carlos led the way to make sure they were following the correct one.

***

Michael wanted to talk to Jennie and secure her agreement to become his mate, but he wasn't convinced she had gotten past their disagreement last night. If he pushed her too soon, she might refuse him again, and that might set his plan back by several days. It was frustrating. Why couldn't she just accept she was lucky to receive such a generous offer, and grab onto it with both hands like almost every other woman he knew would have done?

But this was Jennie, and for some strange reason, he felt proud of her for not just jumping at the chance to be rich. She had a backbone, and she was going to need it if she wanted to earn the respect of his family. His father was the head of their clowder, and he demanded obedience, but he also respected people who made their own decisions and stood up for themselves. At least when it was for the good of the clowder.

Michael had been raised to take over as the head of their clowder after his father, but in order to do that, he had to be mated. His father was still in good health, and Michael had believed it would be many years until he had to find a mate and settle down. But for some reason his father suddenly thought it was time for Michael to prove that he had what it took to become the next head of their clowder. That included, among other things, finding a mate and settling down, and he had been given only six months to do so. It sounded like a lot, but it wasn't when settling down was the last thing he wanted to do.

Michael had spent a couple of months evaluating all potential females of his shifter kind, but they were either too brainwashed, too cold, or too skinny for his liking. So, when Carlos had asked him to join them on this trip with Jennie, it seemed like the perfect solution to his problem. Only he had thought Jennie liked him and that securing her as his mate would be easy. He had three weeks left to get Jennie to accept him, or his father would choose a suitable mate for him, no doubt with the correct political ties. And if he knew his father, the mate he would choose for Michael would be some brainwashed meek creature with the backbone of a worm.

***

As they were nearing the top of the hill, the terrain changed. The ground was littered with rocks, and it was harder to walk. They had to keep a close eye on where they put their feet to avoid stumbling.

Finally arriving at the highest point, Jennie looked around, and the view took her breath away. The small village with its mostly white houses scattered around the tiny harbor. The sea loch with the narrow sound linking it to the sea. And all the islands scattered on the horizon. She understood why people chose to live there, even though it was way out in nowhere.

They rested for a while and had some food. They had only been walking for an hour and a half, and the plan was to reach the next mountaintop behind the one they were on before returning to the cottage. From there they should be able to see the Isle of Skye.

Jennie got up and stretched. She put her backpack back on and as if on cue, they all started walking. Carlos led the way as before, taking them down a steep and rocky track.

It was a bit slow-going, but some of the rocks were loose, and it would be easy to fall if you weren't careful. Jennie was concentrating on the track when she thought she heard someone shouting. It was faint, and she looked around at the others to see if they had heard it as well.

Michael was staring down the hill to the left of the track. "There's someone down there. Perhaps she's hurt."

Before anyone could say anything, he was on his way down in the direction he had been looking. Jennie quickly followed him, and the others changed their direction to follow behind. It was still slow-going with all the rocks, but a few minutes later, Jennie saw a woman lying in between some large boulders. Michael was already there, talking to her. He had moved like a mountain goat down the steep, rocky slope, surefooted and agile.

"She fell and tumbled in between these large rocks, and one of them rolled to trap her leg. Her leg is most likely fractured, and trying to move the rock might end up crushing her leg. She's otherwise okay. No sign of shock or heavy bleeding."

Jennie was impressed. Michael had already assessed the woman's condition and seemed to be in total control of the situation.

"I can't get a signal." Carlos was frowning at his cell phone. "Must be because we're in between these mountains. I'll go back up to the top to try there."

Jennie retrieved her cell phone from her pocket, but she didn't get a signal either. When she looked up toward where Carlos and Marna had started walking up the hill, she was shocked to see they were hardly visible. Thick fog was covering the area. Where had that come from? It had been perfectly clear a minute ago.

"I'll go get help." Jennie looked at the others. "With this fog, they can't airlift anyone in, but I might be able to find someone who can help in the village."

"You'll get lost." Ann was looking at her with wide eyes.

Jennie shook her head. "No, I have a good sense of direction. I'll be fine. I'll follow the track back up to the top. Walking down on the other side, I'll hit the main road at some point, even if my aim at the village is off."

"Be careful." Michael's eyebrows were drawn together in concern.

"I will." Jennie hurried up the steep rocky hillside. It was a good thing she was fit and used to hiking.

∞∞∞

Ever since Trevor had left Jennie on the shore of the sea loch that morning, he had been restless. No matter what he tried to do, his thoughts went back to their night together, and he lost his concentration. He tried taking a nap, but it was no use. Every time he was about to drift off, she was there with him, and his dick hardened enough to wake him.

By midday he had given up on trying to do something useful. Duncan had just told him to leave the shed where he was repairing the roof, for almost knocking him off it.

Trevor went inside the house. He wasn't used to having his emotions knocking him off kilter like this. And all after one night with a beautiful woman. If this continued, he would be a raving lunatic by the end of the week.

He went to his room and shed his clothes before changing into his wolf. Perhaps he would be able to relax in his animal form. Trevor ran down the stairs and out the door. Keeping hidden as much as possible, he trotted over to the stone fence and lay down behind a large tree. He didn't like sleeping inside in his wolf form. Outside, his senses easily kept him informed about what was going on around him, even when he was resting. And as a wolf he belonged in nature, not in a house.

Someone running had him raising his head. It wasn't usually a cause for alarm around there, but the wind was blowing the wrong direction, preventing him from picking up the person's scent.

Then, he heard the gate open and Jennie yelling his name, and before he could think better of it, he bounded over the lawn toward her. She was breathless and sweaty, and looked like she had been running for a while, dust covering her hiking boots and her legs.

Jennie ground to a halt when she saw him. Her face went deathly pale, her eyes widened, and she smelled of fear. Trevor stopped and was suddenly uncertain of what to do. She obviously needed help, but he was in his wolf form, which clearly terrified her.

Just then Duncan came running around the corner of the house, having heard Jennie yelling. Seeing Trevor in his wolf form, he looked confused for a second before his expression hardened into anger.

Stopping close to Trevor, Duncan stared at him. "What the fuck are you doing? Go inside."

That was, of course, the right thing to do. Trevor backed away a couple of steps before turning around and running as fast as he could inside the house and up the stairs. He shifted on his way down the corridor to his room. He found his clothes and shoes and put them on, and then raced back outside.

Jennie and Duncan were still on the lawn, and Jennie was talking. When she saw him, her eyes looked relieved, and he ran over to her and took her hands in his.

"What's going on?"

He could feel Duncan's angry eyes on him, but he didn't have time to care about that when Jennie needed help.

"There's a woman who's hurt up there." Jennie nodded in the direction of the hill behind the village. "Her leg is stuck underneath a bolder and trying to move the boulder might crush her leg."

"One of your friends?" He looked into her eyes and tried to convey calm and confidence.

Jennie shook her head. "No, we found her. She was alone and yelling for help."

"Okay." Trevor looked at Duncan. "We'll help her."

Duncan gave him a short nod of agreement.

Looking back at Jennie, Trevor quickly assessed her condition. "Perhaps you should stay here. You're exhausted."

"No, I'm fine, and I have to show you where she is. You won't be able to find her otherwise." She looked determined. "I can handle it."

Trevor realized there was no point trying to convince her to stay, and he couldn't exactly tell her he would change into a wolf and follow her scent back the way she had come. Finding the woman would be easy for him. "Okay, let's go then."

"I'll find an iron bar to help us move the boulder. Just go. I'll catch up." Duncan started back toward the shed.

Trevor released Jennie's hands and let her take the lead back the way she had come. She ran for a while before slowing to a fast walk. The ascent got gradually steeper, but Jennie pressed on. Trevor was impressed. She was fit and more resilient than he would have given her credit for.

The track was getting rockier and more treacherous, and he kept a keen eye on her to make sure he would be there to catch her if she tripped and fell. The fog was thick, but he had run around this area so many times both in his human and wolf form that he knew exactly where they were.

It was only about two hundred yards left to the top of the hill when Jennie stumbled. He caught her around the waist before she hit the ground.

"Let's take a break, all right? You're pushing yourself too hard." Trevor felt a strong need to pick her up and carry her the rest of the way to the top, but he resisted the urge. He had a feeling Jennie wouldn't be impressed by that.

"I'm fine. Let's continue. I think we're almost at the top."

He sighed. "Jennie, please. You're going to hurt yourself. Then we'll have two people to rescue from up here."

CHAPTER 14

Jennie heard the concern in Trevor's voice and realized he was right. It would be worse for everyone if she fell and broke her leg. And she was pretty worn out. She just couldn't let herself think about that at the moment.

"Okay, but I don't want to stop. I'll slow down, though."

"Good."

They reached the top, and she continued over to the track going down on the other side.

"How far down is she?" Trevor was walking right behind her as she picked her way slowly down the rocky track.

"I guess about three hundred yards."

"Down by the boulders on the left?"

"Yes." Jennie should have known that Trevor would be familiar with these mountains. He would probably have found the place on his own if she had explained where the woman was. And much faster as well. "Just go ahead. I'm not as fast as you are." Hopefully, the woman's condition hadn't deteriorated. It had been more than two hours since Jennie left, and a lot could have happened in that time.

"I'm not leaving you here on this treacherous track on your own in the fog. We'll get there together."

"Trevor, I'll be fine."

"I'm not leaving you. End of discussion." His tone was stern.

Jennie smiled to herself. He was protective of her, and she liked it, but she wasn't going to tell him that.

Trevor insisted on walking beside her and holding her hand the last hundred yards down to the boulders. They were walking off the track, and the ground was littered with loose rocks. No wonder the woman had fallen while walking there, but why would she wander off the track in the first place?

When they arrived, the situation was much the same as when Jennie had left. Michael was sitting close to the woman, holding her hand for support, and the woman was still lying in between two large boulders, one of which was leaning on her right leg just below the knee.

"That's going to be a bitch to move, but we'll do it." Duncan's voice right behind Jennie startled her. He had probably walked behind them for quite a while without her noticing him. That showed how worn out she was. As soon as she stopped, she noticed how exhausted she truly was and sat down.

Trevor and Duncan immediately got to work. Using the iron bar Duncan had brought and smaller rocks to support the boulder, they gradually moved the large boulder off the woman's leg. It didn't take long before the woman was free, and Michael pulled her out from between the boulders.

Duncan offered to carry the woman back to the village, but the woman still hadn't let go of Michael's hand, and Michael insisted he would be fine carrying her. He gently lifted her in his arms and started the climb up to the top.

Jennie put her water bottle back in her backpack and got to her feet. She felt a bit dizzy, but it would probably pass as soon as she got going.

Trevor fell into step beside her as she started up the hill. She tried to keep up with Michael and Duncan. The others had gone ahead and were already swallowed by the fog. Her legs wouldn't have it, though. They felt so heavy and sluggish, and her pace got slower and slower.

"Okay, that's it."

That was all the warning she got, before she was swept up into Trevor's strong arms and cradled against his chest.

"I can walk." But even to herself she didn't sound convincing. "I'm too heavy for you to carry."

He chuckled. "I'm strong if you haven't noticed, and I'm carrying you back to my house whether you want to or not. You're exhausted, and I'm going to take care of you."

"I'm not sure I'm going to be much fun tonight," she whispered.

He just laughed and kept walking.

Jennie felt bad for letting him carry her, but she had a feeling he wouldn't let her walk no matter how much she pleaded or screamed.

She couldn't help dozing off a bit on the way down

to Trevor's house. She heard him talking to the others from time to time but didn't catch what was being said. He held her firmly in his arms the whole way and never stopped to take a break. This guy had to be some kind of superhuman, but then he had proven that the night before.

∞∞∞

Michael watched the ambulance drive away. He kept telling himself Stephanie would be fine, but for some reason he regretted not getting into the ambulance with her. She had begged him to come with her, and he had almost given in, but then he had remembered why he was in Scotland in the first place. He didn't have time to waste on anything other than securing his mate, and Jennie would probably be back later in the evening and need him to take care of her. She had been exhausted, and Trevor had told them he would call a doctor to get her checked out just in case.

The others were talking as they headed down toward the cottage, but Michael wasn't in the mood to join in the conversation. He didn't like that Trevor had taken Jennie to his house, but Michael had been busy at the time, making sure Stephanie settled into the ambulance okay. Knocking on the wolf's door and demanding to take Jennie to the cottage didn't seem like a good idea. It might well backfire and provoke Jennie into saying *no* to him and throwing herself at the wolf instead. That would be a disaster, and he couldn't risk it.

Instead, he would go back to the cottage and prepare for her arrival. He would make sure his room was tidy, and then he would make her a sandwich in case she was hungry when she got back. Jennie would, of course, sleep in his bed so he could keep an eye on her, and after seeing his concern for her wellbeing, she would be happy to accept his offer. Perhaps what had happened would turn out to be his lucky break.

ooooo

She woke up, lying on Trevor's bed while the man himself was gently removing her hiking boots.

"Just relax. I'm going to take off some of your clothes and then you're going to sleep."

Jennie smiled and closed her eyes. If there was a heaven, it had to be like this. A gorgeous guy caring for you, not even wincing when he was removing your dirty socks.

"You think I'm gorgeous? I have to disappoint you, though. You're not in heaven, but I'll remove your dirty socks anytime you need me to."

Jennie opened her eyes and studied Trevor's face as he climbed onto the bed next to her. She hadn't realized she had spoken aloud, but she didn't feel embarrassed about what she had said.

"I think that's the most romantic thing anyone has ever said to me. And, yes, I think you're gorgeous, both on the outside and the inside."

He bent over her and gave her a quick kiss on the lips before sitting up and unzipping her shorts.

"Let's get your clothes off so you can sleep."

She helped him pull off her shorts before sitting up and removing her T-shirt. While she was pulling the T-shirt over her head, she felt Trevor unfasten her bra.

Jennie couldn't help smiling at him when he gently removed her bra. "Sleep, huh?"

"Yes, but I want you naked beside me." He flashed her a grin. "Then I've got something to hold onto while I sleep." His eyes dipped to her breasts, clearly showing his intentions.

He moved off the bed and started removing his clothes. Jennie followed his every movement. Removing his T-shirt revealed his magnificent chest, not to mention his thick shoulders and those perfectly carved abs. It was enough to have any woman drooling. He unbuttoned his shorts and pulled down the zipper. His big cock stood at attention, and she felt her jaw drop.

"Sorry. I can't help it. Having you around does that to me." Trevor gave her a small smile while stepping out of his shorts. "But you need to sleep. Any other activities will have to wait."

"Other activities," she murmured, still staring at his groin.

Trevor came up to the bed and started pulling down the covers. She got underneath them, and Trevor climbed in beside her, pulling her close against his chest. They were spooning, but he kept the lower half of his body separated from hers.

"Now sleep. I'll be here when you wake up, and your friends know I'm taking care of you."

"And by taking care of me, you mean…" Jennie left the sentence hanging.

He chuckled, and she felt his chest vibrating. "Getting you a doctor and making sure you're okay."

"Ah, so you're Doctor Trevor now?"

"Something like that. Now sleep."

"Okay. If it's what the doctor orders."

"It is."

Jennie closed her eyes. Trevor's muscular body behind her and holding her was arousing, but she was truly too tired to get overly excited about having his naked body so close. It didn't take long before she drifted off to sleep.

***

Trevor had a hard time not letting his hands roam the exquisite terrain of Jennie's body, and his dick was as hard as granite from being this close to her. But she needed to relax and sleep, and that was more important.

Jennie had really pushed her body to the limit to get that woman help; any further and she would have been sick. But she would be fine after a proper night's sleep and a big breakfast in the morning.

After a couple of hours lying behind Jennie as she slept, he was getting desperate. His shaft was still like a steel bar, refusing to soften even though he tried to focus on something other than the beautiful woman in his arms. It was impossible, though, with her so close, and the memories of what they had done the night before flashing through his mind.

He carefully removed the arm that was draped along her thigh and rolled over on his back. But trying to remove his other arm from underneath her head was a more complicated operation. Carefully lifting her head, he inched his arm out. Just when he thought he was all clear, Jennie rolled toward him, effectively trapping his arm again. Trevor sighed and decided to wait a few minutes before trying again.

The feel of her hand coming up to caress his chest

had his muscles tensing. When her hand slowly slid down his stomach, he held his breath. Her fingers reached his cock and gripped the head before stroking his shaft from tip to root. Trevor shuddered. Having her touch him like this was both pure agony and exquisite pleasure. His balls were pulled up so tight it almost felt like they were going to explode, but her hand felt so good on him.

Jennie suddenly sat up beside him. "I think we need to do something about this." She gave his cock a squeeze, and his whole body jerked in response.

"You're exhausted." His voice was so rough it didn't even sound like him.

"I'll be the judge of that. Have you been this hard the whole time?"

Trevor nodded. "I can take care of it. You just go back to sleep. I'll be back in a few minutes." He started getting up, but she put her hands on his chest, pushing him back down.

Her eyes were narrow when she looked at him. "You're going to get yourself off? Don't you want me to do it?"

"More than anything, but—"

Before he could say anything more, she yanked the covers off them and straddled his legs. Then she bent forward, and he realized what she intended.

"Jennie." His voice was rough and shaky.

Her lips wrapped around the tip of his cock, and he lost the ability to speak. Her hand gripped the base of his rod, and she slowly inched her lips closer to her hand, taking as much of him as she could into her mouth. Setting a slow pace, she moved up and down him while using her tongue to caress the sensitive area at the front of the head.

Trevor fisted his hands at his sides to prevent himself from moving. He was getting close, and the feel of her other hand gripping his balls gently almost had him spilling his seed. She carefully massaged his balls while continuing her slow pace. Then, she suddenly tightened her lips around him while sucking and swirling her tongue against him. That did it for him. He roared as his cock jerked, shooting into her mouth. The powerful orgasm spread through his body in wave after wave and didn't release him for what felt like minutes.

His breathing was choppy and uneven when he finally came down, and the tension in his muscles started to ease. He opened his eyes to see Jennie grinning down at him.

"I thought you might stay up there for hours. Do you regret not doing it yourself?"

Trevor snorted. "As if. That was amazing. I think I'll allow you to do that again sometime."

Jennie laughed, and before she realized what he intended, he had her on her back, pinned beneath his body.

"Now it's my turn. I can't wait to taste you again."

Jennie tensed. "I'm all sweaty and dirty. I would like to take a shower first."

***

Jennie wouldn't mind having Trevor's mouth on her, but knowing she was covered in dirt and sweat made her uncomfortable.

Trevor gave her a quick kiss on her lips, before she suddenly found herself in his arms on the way to the bathroom.

"Shower it is then, because I want to taste your juicy pussy."

He set her down on her feet in front of the shower stall and reached inside to turn on the water. Then, he bent his head and kissed her. It was a slow and tender kiss, and if she didn't know better, she would have said the kiss was filled with love. They both opened their mouths and let their tongues explore and caress each other's mouths.

Trevor was a fantastic kisser, and Jennie felt lost in him. When he pulled back and looked at her, she realized she was holding on to his muscular ass and his shaft was trying to poke a hole in her abdomen.

He reached up and loosened her braid before pulling her into the shower. Standing underneath the spray felt amazing, and she closed her eyes and just breathed for a little while.

Jennie started when Trevor's mouth latched onto one of her nipples. His hand grabbed her other breast and kneaded it firmly. The budding heat in her lower abdomen started growing, and she gasped when he sucked hard on her nipple, the sensation seeming to move to her clit. He moved his mouth over to her other nipple and gave it the same treatment.

He suddenly stopped and pulled her out of the spray.

"I'm going to wash your hair." It was a statement not a question. He dumped shampoo into his hand and started massaging it into her hair, giving her a firm and thorough scalp massage in the process. It was heaven.

Then he proceeded to wash her whole body, teasing her clit while he was washing her down there.

She started squirming, having trouble standing still with him playing with her like that.

"Rinse off." He let go of her abruptly and started washing his hair.

Jennie scowled at him. "Are you just going to leave me hanging? I was enjoying that."

Trevor chuckled. "I know. And I won't be leaving you alone for long. Have a little patience."

She backed into the spray and rinsed her hair and body. When she was done and she opened her eyes, he was standing in front of her covered in suds from head to toe. As she took a step toward him, he moved to walk around her to get into the spray. But before he got past her, she reached out and gripped his stiff cock firmly at the base.

He froze and his eyes widened in surprise. When Jennie started moving her hand up and down, stroking him firmly, he hissed, and his eyes darkened.

"Jennie, I…"

She gave him what was probably a wicked smile. "Two can play at that game, you know?" Stroking him a bit faster and firmer, she watched as his muscles tensed up. Then she abruptly let him go.

Trevor groaned and glared at her. Then, he stepped into the spray and started rinsing off.

Oops. Maybe she had gone a bit too far. He looked pissed, standing in the shower with his eyes closed.

But before she could do anything about it, he suddenly launched himself at her grabbing the back of her thighs and lifting her against his body. She squeaked in surprise.

They were out the door of the bathroom, and she was airborne. Jennie landed on her back on the bed and before she stopped bouncing, Trevor pulled her thighs apart and started sucking on her sensitive nub. He vibrated his tongue against her clit, and she couldn't help whimpering. The intense pleasure made her try to close her thighs, but he pinned them open using one arm. A finger breached her opening, stroking her channel slowly, and Jennie moaned.

She reached down, slid her fingers into Trevor's wet hair, and held on to him for support. He added another finger inside her and started pumping them faster while licking and sucking on her clit. Jennie was getting close, and her pelvis started moving of its own accord.

Trevor suddenly stopped before moving his mouth to kiss the inside of her thigh tenderly.

"Trevor, please." Her voice was breathy.

She needed to come badly, and she was certain he knew exactly how close she was and was stopping on purpose.

"Do you want me to continue?" The amusement in his voice was distinct.

"Yes, please."

His mouth latched onto her swollen clit, and his fingers pumped fast inside her. He bit down gently on her nub, and she soared as pleasure raced through her body.

When she could breathe again, Trevor was putting on a condom, and then he rose up above her. She suddenly felt her body spinning, and she landed on her front on the bed. He gripped her hips and lifted her up on her knees. His cock nudged her opening, before he drove into her to the hilt in one swift movement. Jennie screamed. It felt so good having him stretch her pussy and settle deep inside her. He leaned over her back and his fingers found her nub. She was still sensitive from just coming and tried to move away from his touch, but his body locked her in place.

He started moving in and out of her using long fast strokes, supporting his weight on one hand planted beside hers. Jennie soon found herself well underway to another orgasm, and judging by the sounds he was making, Trevor wasn't far off either. He was snarling close to her ear as he pumped into her faster and faster, his pace starting to break up a bit. Pleasurable heat was radiating from her lower abdomen, the movement of Trevor's rod and fingers stoking the fire within her into an intense blaze racing through her body, making her scream and shake. Trevor's cock started jumping inside her, bringing the pleasure to an even higher level. It seemed to go on for a long time before they both came down, panting in unison.

Trevor gently tipped them over onto their sides on the bed. Kissing her neck gently, he stroked her thigh with his large hand.

"That was amazing." His voice was rough. "I might have to chain you to my bed, so you'll stay longer than a few days."

Jennie smiled. Some people might think that sounded scary, but to her it sounded wonderful, at least with a man like Trevor.

She tried to speak but was interrupted by a huge yawn.

"Right. You need to sleep." Trevor pulled out of her and tucked the covers around her body, before he went to the bathroom to take off the condom.

He came back and crept in behind her, pulling her

firmly against his body and putting his leg over hers. It was like he wanted to be her human shield, putting himself between her and the world to protect her.

CHAPTER 15

Trevor woke when Jennie turned around, burying her face against his chest. Sneaking a peek at his watch, he saw it was seven o'clock in the morning. They had been sleeping for hours. She still slept peacefully, and he held her close to him for a while, enjoying the feel of her smaller body against his bigger one.

He reached up and combed through her long blond hair with his fingers. Jennie was beautiful, but that wasn't the only thing that drew him to her. She was a strong person and more than capable of standing up to him. He needed that in his mate.

Trevor froze. Jennie couldn't be his mate. She wasn't a wolf, not even a shifter, and she had no idea his kind existed. He cringed when he remembered her reaction to his wolf. She hadn't just been a little afraid; she had been terrified. How would she react if she found out Trevor was a wolf? Would she still be terrified of his animal form? Or even worse, would she be terrified of him in human form as well, knowing he could turn into a wolf?

Well, he wasn't going to find out, so there was no point worrying about it. She was his for a few more nights only, and then she was leaving. It was for the best and would give him an opportunity to search for an alpha female to take as a mate. The thought left him frigid, though. Just the thought of someone other than Jennie in his bed felt wrong.

He would go and speak to Hamish and Ildri later. It wouldn't change his situation, but at least he would know more about the relationship between a wolf and a human.

"What are you thinking about? You look so serious." Jennie had woken up and was studying his face.

He smiled at her. "Nothing particular." Trevor didn't like lying, but this wasn't something he could discuss with her. "We should get up. Your friends will be waiting soon. Why don't you take a shower while I fix us breakfast?"

Jennie sighed. "Okay, I guess it's time. No more hanky panky until tonight." She shot him a grin over her shoulder as she sat up and got out of bed.

He watched her as she walked to the bathroom door and opened it. Her ass was perfection, and he couldn't wait to take her back to bed. His shaft was rock hard, but he made sure to keep it hidden under the covers, or they wouldn't be getting out of bed anytime soon.

In the bathroom doorway, she turned around. One of her eyebrows was raised, and she put her hands on her hips. "Are you checking me out?"

Trevor laughed and nodded. "Absolutely. I could

watch you sashaying naked over my floor all day."

The corners of her mouth tilted upward in a small smile as she narrowed her eyes. "Are you certain that's all you'd want to do? I've got a feeling that wouldn't be enough for long."

"You've got me there. Now, go take that shower before I find some rope and tie you to my bed for the day. I have a lot of ideas on how to keep you busy for hours."

Jennie laughed and walked into the bathroom, closing the door behind her.

He got up and dressed before heading off to the kitchen. Focusing on Jennie's need for food made his still-hard dick start softening.

Duncan was nowhere to be seen. Either he was still sleeping, or he was out working. Even when he spent the night with a woman, he was always back early in the morning. And if that was because he felt an obligation to start work early in the morning, or if it had something to do with him not wanting to give the woman the wrong impression, Trevor had no idea.

After searching through the fridge and the pantry, he pulled out the ingredients for a full English breakfast. That should replace some of the energy Jennie had used the day before.

He heard her coming down the stairs and approaching the kitchen. Turning around to give her a smile as she walked into the kitchen, he froze when he saw the fear in her eyes. She was looking around the kitchen like she was expecting something horrible to jump out at her at any moment.

"Jennie, what's wrong?" He strode toward her, wanting more than anything to make her feel safe.

"Is your dog outside?"

He winced when he realized why she was scared. "You don't have to worry about him. He would never hurt you."

"I'm not so sure. He looked like he was going to attack yesterday. If Duncan hadn't shown up when he did…" She trailed off and looked down.

"I'm really sorry he scared you, Jennie, but he's very good at picking up emotions. He probably sensed your distress when you came in through the gate and thought you needed protection." That was true at least. He would try to stick to the truth as much as possible.

"Really?" She looked suspicious when she raised her eyes to his. "Why would he want to protect someone he doesn't even know?"

"He'll protect anyone he considers less powerful than himself, unless there's a good reason not to. He doesn't attack people. Especially not harmless females."

Jennie didn't look like she believed him, but she didn't say anything.

He went to check on the food he was making. Turning to her, he smiled. "Would you mind setting the table?"

She nodded and started looking through the cupboards and drawers to find what they needed. Trevor intentionally didn't tell her where to find things. He wanted her to get to know her way around his house on her own, to make her feel at home there.

He brought the food to the table, and they sat down.

"Have you had a full English breakfast before?"

She shook her head. "I don't think so."

"Well, it's bacon, eggs, sausage, baked beans, hash browns, black pudding, and toast. There are other varieties, but this is the way I usually make it. I'm not English, so I've probably taken some liberties with how I cook it. Perhaps my version should be called a full American-English breakfast or something like that."

"It smells good. I'm hungry." Jennie smiled at him. "Thank you for making me breakfast."

He chuckled. "Don't thank me until you've tasted it."

They ate, and to his delight, Jennie appeared to enjoy his food. It felt good providing for her, making sure she remained healthy and happy. He couldn't let her fear of dogs go, though.

"What happened to make you so scared of dogs?"

Her face stiffened in fear again, and he really detested that look on her face. It set his protective instincts on high alert.

"I was attacked by the neighbor's dog when I was six years old. It was a big shaggy black dog, and everyone was telling me how friendly it was. I remember it growling viciously at me before attacking. The bite wasn't bad. I don't have a physical scar, but that episode is stuck in my brain. I can tolerate small dogs quite well, like the kind some people carry around in their purse. But big dogs terrify me, so I make sure to stay away from them."

"Do you remember anything about what happened prior to the dog attacking you? If a dog attacks like that, it's usually because it feels threatened."

"I can't recall the circumstances leading up to the attack. It's just the growling and the way the dog launched itself at me that I remember."

"Maybe you should ask your parents or whoever else was there at the time. It might shed some light on why it happened and help you understand the dog's actions. It might even help you to overcome your fear." He really wanted to help her, not just for himself but for her. Being overcome by fear like that must be horrible. Trevor didn't think he had ever experienced terror like he had witnessed on Jennie's face.

Jennie lowered her gaze to her plate. "My parents are dead. But even if they weren't, they wouldn't have been able to help. There was nobody else around when it happened. Apparently, I'd just gotten off the school bus, and I was walking past the neighbor's yard when the dog came at me. The neighbor heard the growling and my screams and came out to grab the dog."

Trevor felt like an ass. Not only had he made her go into the details of the dog incident from her childhood, but he had made her remember the loss of her parents. *Way to go, Trevor.* He was certainly making a good impression this morning.

He reached out and took her hand in his. "I'm sorry about your parents, Jennie. I didn't know. It was careless of me to bring them up."

She met his eyes and gave him a small smile. "It's okay. It's not like it was your fault. They died when I was eighteen in a plane crash. I don't have any siblings, but I've got good friends who have helped and supported me. And my parents left me the house and enough money to get me through college. It could've been worse."

Trevor's need to protect and provide for her upped a level, and he had to stop himself from proposing to take care of her. Jennie was an independent woman who was used to taking care of herself. He didn't think him butting into her life and trying to take control would be welcomed by her. She might even reject him completely.

"You're a strong woman, Jennie. I admire that. And a sexy one."

Jennie smiled and raised an eyebrow at him. "Trying for favors, are you?"

He barked out a laugh. "Absolutely, favors from you are most welcome. Shall I pick you up tonight at the same time?"

Jennie looked like she was trying for a moderate smile, but then it widened into a toothy grin. "Yes, I'd love that." She blushed. "I mean… You know what I mean."

Chuckling, he rose from the table and gathered their plates. "That blush is most becoming. I wouldn't mind seeing that more often."

They helped each other put the dishes in the dish washer, before Trevor followed Jennie out the backdoor.

"Oh, I forgot to ask about the woman who was hurt." Her eyes were wide when she looked up at him. "I guess I've been a bit preoccupied. What happened to her yesterday? Was she taken to the hospital?"

Trevor nodded. "Yes, your friends managed to get ahold of the emergency services on the way down, so the ambulance was waiting here when we arrived. She seemed fine apart from her leg. Hopefully, the fracture isn't too complicated to be set properly, but being young, she'll probably make a full recovery."

"Thank goodness. I was afraid the time I took

getting her help might've made her injuries worse."

Trevor put his hand on her lower back to comfort her. At least that was the excuse he gave himself for touching her.

"No, don't worry about that. You did everything you could, Jennie. She's in your and your friends' debt. Without you she could've died up there. I never asked what she was doing up there alone, wandering around off the track. That's never a good idea."

Jennie shook her head. "I was wondering the same thing. It's an odd thing to do, walking around alone in terrain like that in a remote area. Perhaps she's from a village nearby and knows the area well. It might just have been an unfortunate accident."

"No, I think I would've recognized her if she was local. I know practically everyone within twenty miles of here, at least their faces, but I've never seen her before." Trevor couldn't exactly tell Jennie he had been close enough to the woman to pick up her scent while moving the boulder. He knew for a fact she wasn't from this area. While in his wolf form, he had roamed around all the villages within at least a twenty-mile radius, and he had crisscrossed the mountains, but he had never picked up her scent anywhere.

"I hope she's more careful in the future. Hopefully, she's learned from this incident that it's not safe to go hiking by yourself in areas like this."

"I'm sure she has."

Jennie suddenly stopped, and Trevor turned to her.

"There's something I've been meaning to tell you, but I've never gotten around to it."

Trevor felt the apprehension sink its ice-cold claws into his spine. He didn't like the sound of that.

"Okay. What is it?" He knew she hadn't been intimate with another man recently, because being so close to her he would have smelled him on her. Unless they hadn't been together for a couple of months. Humans didn't mate like shifters did, so they didn't carry the scent of their partner for more than a couple of months. What if she was promised to someone, and Trevor was her one last taste of freedom before getting married? It shouldn't matter to him, since he wasn't going to see her after this week, but the anger and hurt building inside him told him he cared more than he should.

"On Sunday when we went for a walk along the shore, we met three unpleasant men. Or unpleasant is putting it too mildly. They were downright rude and threatening."

He felt the relief zing through him, and he wanted to laugh. That would be the wrong thing to do, though, and he tried to look serious. And thinking about it, he was wondering who had behaved like that toward Jennie and her friends.

"What happened?"

"They told my friends to leave even though we're renting a cottage from a local family, but for some reason, I was allowed to stay. They said that this is wolf territory. Is that a local motorcycle club or something?"

Trevor had been waiting for something like that to happen, so he wasn't surprised. He wasn't sure who had targeted Jennie's friends, but they were obviously werewolves. "They're just some local assholes not very friendly toward tourists. Did they hurt any of you?"

"No, I asked if they knew you, and that had a

profound effect. I've never seen anyone go from aggressive to scared and apologizing so fast. I hope you don't mind my mentioning your name. Are you some kind of local godfather or something?"

He couldn't help laughing. "Oh, yes. They know I'll hurt them for threatening someone I know." Then he became serious. "No, but my family has been supporting this community for generations, and the locals don't take kindly to people who hurt us, even indirectly."

Jennie nodded. "I don't think they'll bother us again, so I'm not concerned, but I wanted you to know."

"I appreciate it. And please tell me if anything else happens."

"I will."

They continued down the track and were soon on the shore of the sea loch close to the path up to the cottage. Trevor turned Jennie toward him, and before she could say anything, he pulled her close and kissed her. He didn't want to let her go, even for the day, but he couldn't tell her that. It might scare her away. Their agreement was for sex while she was there, and no further commitment was included.

CHAPTER 16

Trevor kissed her like he would never see her again. It was intense and passionate and longing, like he didn't want to let her go, even for the day.

Jennie felt the same way, and she answered his kiss with the same passion and longing. It was crazy after such a short time, but there was no doubt she was falling for him.

They were both breathless and horny by the time they managed to pull away from each other. Trevor's erect cock was making the material of his pants strain to keep it contained, and she couldn't help smiling when she looked at his groin.

"My eyes are up here." His voice was deep and rough.

She laughed and met his eyes. They were filled with amusement.

"At least you have an extra leg to support you on your way back to your house."

He groaned. "I'm going to be labeled a pervert if

anyone sees me in this condition."

Jennie snorted. "Yeah, you'd better not scare a little old lady on your way home. She might beat you up with her umbrella, unless she decides to invite you to her house instead."

Trevor just lifted an eyebrow at her. "That just gave me a whole new perspective on the *Little Red Riding Hood* story."

"What do you mean?" She frowned, not sure what he meant by that.

Trevor shook his head. "Never mind. You should probably go see what your friends are up to. What are your plans for today?"

Jennie didn't want to ask again what he'd meant by the *Little Red Riding Hood* comment, so she let it go. "I'm not sure. I guess I'll find out what they've planned in a few minutes. See you at ten thirty tonight?"

He grinned. "Can't wait." Trevor looked down at his crotch for a second and sighed before meeting her eyes again. "I'll see you then."

Jennie turned around and walked up the path toward the cottage. She was in trouble. Leaving Trevor at the end of the week was going to be extremely difficult, perhaps even break her heart. But that did nothing to deter her from wanting to spend more time with him while she was there. She was going to make the most of the time they had left together, no matter if she was going to suffer for a long time afterward.

ooooo

Michael was pacing in his room. He was furious. It

was eight thirty in the morning, and Jennie still wasn't back. What was she playing at staying the night at another man's house? That kind of behavior was completely unacceptable, even if she was only sleeping in one of Trevor's guestrooms.

He wanted to break something or shift or both, but he couldn't. His rage was about to take over, but he had to force it back. It was important that he had a clear head when Jennie came back, so he could talk to her in a calm and collected manner. Michael had to know what had happened while she was at the bastard's house, and the only way to achieve that was by acting like everything was fine. Otherwise, she would get pissed off and tell him nothing.

∞∞∞

Jennie unlocked the door to her room and entered before closing it behind her. She quickly changed her clothes and brushed her hair. They had gotten a good night's sleep last night, and even though she had been exhausted the night before, she felt refreshed and ready for new adventures this morning.

She walked out of her room and almost crashed into Michael coming around the corner. Anger seemed to flash across his face, but it was gone so quickly she might have misread his expression.

"I'm sorry." Jennie stepped back and smiled at him. "Maybe I should start singing before I reach the corner from now on to avoid an accident."

Michael smiled, but it didn't quite reach his eyes. "So, have you been back long? I was just going to look for you. We're about to have breakfast."

"I just got back actually. How did it go with the woman yesterday? Did the paramedics say anything about her condition and if she's going to be okay? I sort of passed out on the way down the hill. Trevor told me this morning that the ambulance picked her up and took her to the hospital."

"She'll probably be fine once they reset the bones in her leg. She didn't show signs of any other trauma. Are you okay? Did you sleep all right?" His eyes suddenly changed color, going from his normal light brown to almost yellow before reverting to brown.

Jennie frowned and looked away. She must still be a bit tired from the day before. That was probably why she was hallucinating. Or it had just been a trick of the light. "I slept really well, and I feel good. Thank you for asking. Perhaps we should go inside to the others."

She started walking, and Michael fell into step beside her. He didn't say anything, and she was a bit wary of looking into his eyes again in case the same thing happened.

When they entered the kitchen, Ann and Marna both rushed to her and gave her a hug.

"Are you okay?" Ann looked her over with a concerned expression on her face.

"We've been worried about you." Marna took her hand in both of hers. "But we figured Trevor would take good care of you." A small smile played on Marna's lips, and there was a question in her eyes.

Jennie wasn't going to take the bait. At least not with Michael listening. She was quite sure he was going to react badly if she let slip just how well Trevor had taken care of her.

"I'm fine. All I needed was a good night's sleep. My

legs aren't even as sore as I thought they'd be from climbing the hill as fast as I could."

"Are you joining us for breakfast, or have you already eaten?" Judging by Ann's teasing smile she was trying to provoke Jennie into spilling more details of her stay at Trevor's house, but she wasn't going to reveal more than necessary.

"Thank you, but I've already had breakfast. I'd love some coffee, though." Jennie kept an easy smile on her face and didn't give anything away.

Marna was quick to pour her a steaming cup of coffee, and Jennie sat down at the table and sighed in contentment as she took the first sip.

"So, what have you guys planned for today?"

Ann frowned. "We weren't sure how you were going to feel today, so we came up with a couple of easy options. If you aren't up to do much, we thought we'd just stay here and have a lazy day talking and eating chocolate. Or, if you felt okay, we'd take the train to Fort William and have a look around. What do you think? The guys will go hiking, so it'll only be us girls."

Jennie smiled and did a mental fist pump. She wouldn't have to spend the day with Michael. "Fort William sounds perfect, unless you'd rather stay here?"

Both Ann and Marna grinned.

"Fort William, here we come," Marna said before glancing at her watch. "But then we'd better hurry. The train leaves in half an hour."

***

Michael breathed out a sigh of relief. He hadn't been too keen on going hiking and leaving Jennie at the cottage, where Trevor would have access to her if he decided to check on her during the day. In Fort William with the other women, the chance of her running into the bastard was slim. The last thing Michael needed was for Jennie to spend more time with the wolf and choose him over Michael.

He had to think of some excuse to spend time with her this evening so he could convince her to accept his offer. Jennie had everything to gain from becoming his mate, and she would understand that when he explained all the advantages in more detail.

For some reason an image of Stephanie popped into his head, and he wondered how she was doing. She had been so scared and had begged him to come with her in the ambulance. Michael had assumed it was because of her injury. Some people had a fear of hospitals. But thinking about it later, he got the feeling it was something else that had her terrified. He just wasn't sure what it could be.

Michael didn't know which hospital they had taken her to, but he would find out. There was probably one in Fort William.

The women were getting up to leave, and Michael quickly escaped the kitchen and went to his bedroom. He did a search on his phone and found out there was a hospital in Fort William. That was probably where they had taken Stephanie. He was about to click on their phone number to call them when he abruptly stopped.

What was he doing? Why was he so eager to find out how the woman was doing? It wasn't like she was important to him. And by this time, she was most likely surrounded by doting family members and had forgotten all about him.

A strange pain in his chest had him wondering if he was coming down with something, which was unusual, him being a shifter and all. But it quickly disappeared, and he went back to the kitchen to help with the dishes.

∞∞∞

The three of them settled around a table on the train. Jennie was looking forward to exploring Fort William. It was a fairly small town, but it was a lot bigger than the tiny village of Fearolc.

"So." Ann leaned across the table, looking at her intently. "Tell us what happened with Trevor."

Jennie glanced at the other passengers sitting close to them, but they all seemed to be tourists that would have no idea of whom they were speaking.

She looked at Ann across the table and then at Marna, who was sitting next to Jennie. A huge grin spread across Jennie's face, and the girls started laughing.

"I knew it." Ann was shaking her head slowly. "I just knew it. Any good?"

Jennie nodded. "Amazing. Best I've ever had. Even better than any fantasy I've ever had."

"Good. You deserve it." Marna was smiling widely at her. "Are you going to see him again?"

"Yes, he's picking me up at ten thirty tonight." Jennie stopped smiling. "Don't tell Michael, though. I think he'd be really angry. He practically asked me to marry him the day before yesterday, and then he accused me of tipping my kayak on purpose to get Trevor's attention."

Ann and Marna both stared at her in shock.

"What?" Ann's eyes were wide. "But did you tell him that you don't like him that way?"

"I told him that I'm not in love with him, and that I was sorry if he had somehow gotten that impression. But he didn't accept that as a no. He told me it didn't matter because what he could give me would compensate for my lack of feelings. I was too shocked to say anything after that, so he left me alone, saying that he'd leave me to think about it."

Ann shook her head in apparent disbelief. "How can he completely disregard your feelings? Wanting to marry someone who doesn't care about him is a bit weird. As far as I've seen he's quite popular with the ladies, so finding someone nice who wants to marry him shouldn't be that difficult."

"He hasn't brought it up again after that?" Marna was frowning.

"No, but he hasn't really had an opportunity to speak to me alone with everything that happened yesterday. I'm sure he'll approach me later today or tomorrow, and I'll have to tell him in no uncertain terms that there's no way I'm going to marry him." Jennie sighed. "I feel like I've tried to make it clear to him that I don't want him several times already, but it only makes him more persistent in his efforts. I don't understand why he wants to marry me when he knows that I don't care about him. We don't even get along that well."

"Do you want us to talk to James and Carlos?" Ann was looking concerned. "They might be able to get Michael to stop pursuing you and preventing you from enjoying your vacation."

"Yes, I'm sure Carlos would, if not happily talk to him, at least feel it's appropriate to talk to Michael about this." Marna was looking a bit worried. "This borders on harassment."

"Thank you." Jennie felt better after sharing this with her friends. "But let's wait and see what Michael chooses to do next. If he accepts my refusal, I'm just going to forget this ever happened."

"Be sure to tell us if he doesn't give up, though." Ann smiled at her encouragingly. "Our men will help him see reason and not bother you again."

Jennie laughed. "You make it sound like they'd beat him up or something."

A look passed between Ann and Marna before they started laughing as well. It sounded a bit forced, like they actually weren't sure whether the guys would fight or not. That couldn't be right, though. Jennie had never gotten the impression that James and Carlos were likely to resort to violence to resolve a conflict.

CHAPTER 17

After walking Jennie back to the Miller's cottage, Trevor had spent some time walking the fence around the area where he kept his sheep and checking on the animals to make sure they were all healthy. He did this regularly when he stayed in Fearolc. Sheep could easily hurt themselves in the uneven terrain, and he enjoyed the fresh air and lack of human noise. As he was crossing the lawn toward the back of his house, Duncan opened the back door and stood there waiting.

Trevor got the feeling that something was up, but Duncan's expression didn't give anything away.

Duncan stepped back to let him enter. "We have visitors." His tone was low.

Trevor frowned. "Who?" Duncan didn't seem happy about it, which didn't bode well.

"The cats."

That was a surprise. Why on earth would they want to visit a wolf's house? Unless it had something to do with what happened the day before. That was probably it.

"And the women?"

Duncan shook his head. "No, just the cats."

Trevor followed Duncan into the kitchen. The three guys were sitting on one side of the kitchen table. Their expressions were serious. Whatever this visit was about, it wasn't a friendly social call.

"What can we do for you?" Trevor stood facing the three at the table. He wouldn't sit down until he knew why they had come. Duncan had stopped just inside the door to the kitchen, standing there like a silent sentry.

"We want to thank you for helping us yesterday." James was looking at Trevor as he spoke. He was the most dominant of the three males. They had been introduced the day before while walking back down the hill, so Trevor was aware of who was whom of the three felines.

"We realize that it might feel like we're intruding on your territory, but we had no idea this was wolf country when we booked the cottage."

"That's okay. I'm not concerned about that. Jennie told me this morning about the three idiots who confronted you the other day. I'll try to prevent something like that from happening again while you're here." Trevor realized what he was saying gave them the impression that he was the pack master in the area, but it might be better that way. The wolves in this area didn't have a pack master, and that usually wasn't a problem since the families there were all related to each other and typically a peaceful lot. But having other shifters coming into their area had provoked some of the locals to take action. It would be better if the cats believed him to be the pack master. Then they would come to him if something else happened, and it would help him keep Jennie safe. She had no idea of the danger she would be in if there was ever a fight. Being human, she would take a long time to heal from any injuries. Or even worse she could get killed.

"Thank you for that. We'll be leaving on Saturday, so it won't be for much longer. There is, however, another matter that we need to discuss with you." James didn't look happy about it, and Trevor felt his apprehension increase.

"Okay."

James glanced at Michael before fixing his eyes on Trevor. "Jennie is soon to be Michael's mate, and it's not appropriate for her to spend time at another shifter's house without her future mate being present."

The shock raked its icy fingers down Trevor's spine, and he almost winced. By sheer force of will he kept his expression passive, even though he wanted to scream with rage and frustration. Thank fuck he wasn't standing close enough for the cats to scent his distress. What James was saying couldn't be right, though. Jennie would have told him. It had to be some kind of mistake. For one, she would have to know about shifters to agree to become someone's mate, and she obviously didn't. And secondly, she wasn't the type of woman to spend the night with a man if she was about to mate another. He was sure of that.

Trevor folded his arms across his chest. Narrowing his eyes in suspicion, he shifted his gaze to Michael. "How come she doesn't know about shifters if she has agreed to become your mate?"

James answered instead of Michael. "There are a few things she needs to be told before it can be made official, but after tonight it should be settled. We just wanted to make it known to you now to ensure that there could be no misunderstanding as to her status. I realize that this is probably entirely unnecessary, and we appreciate your kindness in caring for her wellbeing last night."

James started to get up, but Trevor wasn't going to let Jennie go that easily. It still didn't add up.

He looked at Michael. "How come you didn't let someone else carry the woman with the broken leg down the mountain yesterday, when your soon-to-be mate obviously needed you? Jennie was exhausted. By sheer luck she didn't get sick after what she put herself through yesterday."

Michael's eyes flashed yellow. It was clear he didn't appreciate what Trevor was saying. James was the one who answered Trevor's question, though.

"I don't think Jennie would ever object to Michael helping someone else, even if it was detrimental to her own health, but that's for Michael and Jennie to discuss."

James had him there. Jennie was a kind and caring person, and she would give up a lot to help someone else, even someone she didn't know. Trevor remembered the way she had staggered as she hurried as fast as she could up the hill to make sure they got to the woman as fast as possible, and he regretted not insisting on Jennie staying at his house while they went to rescue the woman. Maybe he hadn't taken any better care of Jennie than Michael had.

And perhaps this was all for the best. He couldn't

mate Jennie, anyway. He didn't want to lose out on the nights they had planned to spend together while she was there, but spending more time with her would only make it harder to let her go.

But Trevor didn't like Michael, and the thought of him and Jennie together was threatening to send Trevor into a jealous rage. Why would she agree to mate Michael? Or she probably thought of it as marriage since she didn't know about shifters yet. But still? And why hadn't they had sex if she had agreed to marry him? Was it a marriage of convenience? That would explain why she felt it was okay to have sex with someone else. He couldn't imagine Jennie agreeing to a marriage like that, but having already been through a divorce, she might not believe in love anymore. It would explain why she had wanted to meet him down by the shore where nobody could see them. Michael wasn't supposed to know she was sleeping with someone else.

Staring at Michael, Trevor let his wolf bleed into his eyes. "You'd better treat her right. If I ever hear differently, I'll come for you, and there won't be anything left to salvage." Trevor turned around and quickly strode out of the kitchen before he could do something he would regret. "Show our guests out," he said to Duncan as he walked past him.

ooooo

They arrived in Fort William after about an hour on the train. It was beautifully settled in the north end of Loch Linnhe, which was actually a fjord and not a lake, with Ben Nevis right behind keeping a watchful eye over the town and the surrounding area.

They walked along High Street and just absorbed the atmosphere. There were shops and restaurants, and a lot of tourists were milling around, looking to be from all corners of the world.

A sign pointed them in the direction of the West Highland Museum, and without having to exchange any words, they automatically steered toward it. It was always interesting to get a feel for the history of a place. Quite often the past could give you a clue as to the mentality of the modern people living there.

They looked through several of the collections, and Jennie was about to suggest they find a place to have lunch when she spotted a painting of a wolf in a corner. The animal was light gray, with dark-gray markings on its head and along its spine. Standing beneath a tree, it was staring at something happening to the left of the picture frame.

Jennie found herself standing right in front of the painting, staring in fascination at the creature. Why was she so sure it was a wolf? It could be a dog. But for some reason, she was sure that the light-gray canine was a wolf.

Finally managing to tear her eyes from the beautiful animal, she looked around at the other artifacts in the corner. There was a wolf trap on display and a description of how it was used. Apparently, it had been used in the 1850s to try to catch a wolf that had been sighted by several people in the Glenfinnan area, a little west of Fort William.

An old book lying open in a display case showed a small drawing of a wolf changing into a man, and there was an account of how some of these wolfmen were believed to inhabit an area of the Highlands between Fort William and the Isle of Skye. The drawing was fascinating, showing the various stages of transformation from wolf to man.

An image of Trevor's dog suddenly popped into Jennie's head, and she frowned. She had been absolutely terrified when the huge beast had bounded toward her across the lawn. It had seemed angry, but thinking back, she remembered getting the feeling it wanted to know what was wrong. There had been something in its eyes, some kind of understanding like it knew she needed help. Which was clearly just proof she had been distressed at the time, since an animal couldn't express those kinds of emotions.

She had no trouble understanding that people believed in the wolfman, though, if they had dogs like that in the Highlands back in the day. People had a lot of imagination back then, perhaps more than modern people who were too busy watching YouTube to spend time exploring their brain's capacity for making stories and being creative.

"Do you want to get something to eat?" Ann's voice right behind her made Jennie jump.

She smiled and turned to face Ann. "Yes, I'm hungry. Let's go."

They found a nice little pub that served food a bit farther down the street, and the three of them settled at a table in the back corner. The place was cozy, and they ordered glasses of wine to drink while they waited for their food.

The conversation circled around their plans for the autumn, but Jennie soon found her mind wandering back to the painting of the wolf and the old book describing the wolfman. She wanted to know more. There had to be more stories about the creature that was supposed to have roamed an area not far from there.

After finishing their meal, they had a look around the shops. There were quite a few souvenir shops and stores, obviously catering to all the tourists, but there were a few clothing stores and a bookshop, as well.

Jennie ended up buying a pale green summer dress with a short, flared skirt. The neckline was deep in the back, plunging almost to her waist. Hopefully Trevor would like it. Looking at the dresses in the store, she found herself evaluating each one based on what she thought Trevor would like. She knew it was stupid, since he was only her vacation fling, but she couldn't help the way she felt.

Wandering down the street later, Jennie suddenly spotted a sign for the local library. Once again she thought of the wolfman. If there was going to be a place where she could find out more about the local folklore, it was going to be the local library.

Jennie agreed to meet her friends at the train station in an hour and hurried down the side street toward the library. It wasn't big by any standards, and she soon found a librarian, who pointed her in the right direction.

After grabbing a few of the oldest volumes she could find, she started flicking through them. The first two didn't mention the wolfman or any creature that could change into a human form. In the third, there was a paragraph mentioning the apparent wolfman sightings, but there were no details. By the time Jennie moved on to the fourth book, she was starting to lose hope of finding any more details. Berating herself for not asking at the museum if they had other materials that were not on display, she started leafing through the book.

There was a lot about old Celtic beliefs and the Loch Ness monster, and she was just about to snap the book shut when she saw the picture of the light-gray wolf. It was the same painting as the one hanging in the museum, and the book had pictures of two other paintings by the same artist. In one the same light-gray wolf, or at least she assumed it was the same, was hiding in between the trees, looking directly at the painter. And in the second an almost black wolf was standing with its head low to the ground and staring at something to the right of the painting.

The book went on to describe the local belief in the wolfman. The creature was supposed to be able to change between its canine form and its human form at will. While it was in its human form, it was impossible to distinguish it from other humans, making it easy for the wolfman to hide its nature. There weren't a lot of reported sightings, but those that were documented specified the human form to be a man. And not just any man, but a particularly tall, muscular, and handsome man.

Jennie's thoughts immediately went to Trevor. He was tall, muscular, and handsome, all right. Or more accurately he was downright gorgeous.

There were other traits linked to the wolfman in its human form, like superhuman strength and stamina, and speed and agility far surpassing any normal human.

The way Trevor had carried her down the hill came

to mind, not to mention his stamina in bed. Yes, strength and stamina—check.

On the next page of the book, there was a map showing all the reported sightings of the wolfman. They were all located to the west of Fort William.

Jennie felt her heart rate elevate. There were two sightings close to Fearolc, and the text below the map spoke of Fearolc and how this was the Gaelic term for werewolf. It went on to say that the origin of the name was uncertain, but it seemed to date back to a time before the first sightings were documented. Whether that meant there had been sightings in that area before the ones that were recorded, and that those early sightings had given rise to the name, was unknown.

There was suddenly a certain logic to the threatening guys on the beach calling the area wolf country. Their motorcycle club, or whatever group they belonged to, probably based its identity on the old local folklore. Not exactly an uncommon thing to do.

Checking her watch, Jennie was surprised to see it was only ten minutes until she was due to meet her friends at the train station. She quickly scanned through the next few pages of the book, but there didn't seem to be anything more written about werewolves. After returning the books to the librarian, she rushed out and down the street to the train station, arriving there with only two minutes to spare before the departure of the train back to Fearolc.

"We thought you might've gotten lost and were preparing a search party." Ann was smiling at Jennie as she came toward her, carrying several shopping bags.

Marna walked beside Ann, and her grin was just as big. "I found this candy shop selling at least twenty different kinds of fudge and caramels."

"Of course you did." Jennie chuckled. If there was one thing that could make Marna happy, it was caramels.

They boarded the train and found their places around a small table. As the train started moving away from Fort William, Jennie couldn't help keeping an eye out for any sign of a wolf in between the trees.

"Did you find any interesting books at the library?" Ann's voice snapped her out of her staring at the landscape outside the window.

Jennie met Ann's gaze and smiled. "As a matter of fact, I did. Do you know what Fearolc really means?"

Ann shook her head. "No, but I'm fairly certain you're about to tell us."

"It means werewolf. Apparently, there have been several werewolf sightings in this area back in the day. Even two separate reports of werewolves being seen in Fearolc."

Ann and Marna both stared at her without saying anything.

"Isn't it fascinating?" Jennie looked at her friends excitedly. "I love folklore. It gives such a unique take on the history of a place and the people who live there.

"Sure." Marna gave her a quick smile, before diving into one of her shopping bags. "Here. Try one of these." She pulled out a huge bag of fudge and placed it on the table between them. "Why wait until we get back to the cottage, right? Once my husband gets a taste of these, it won't take long before there are only crumbs left."

"Yeah." Ann grinned. "We'd better secure our share now before we get competition."

Jennie was left feeling a bit like her friends had just brushed her off. Normally, they liked to discuss folklore and stories, so it seemed a bit strange they had changed the subject so fast without showing any interest in her discovery. Then again, perhaps she was reading too much into their behavior. Both Ann and Marna had a point about their husbands. Sweets had a tendency to disappear almost instantly around those guys.

CHAPTER 18

Trevor was driving way too fast, skidding around the tight curves on the narrow road. His reflexes were better than a human's, but it wasn't a good excuse for driving like a lunatic. His black mood was, though.

He still couldn't believe Jennie was going to marry that bastard of a cat. It just didn't make sense. Trevor was normally quite a good judge of a person's character, and Jennie just wasn't the type of woman to deliberately betray someone. He had a hard time believing she would have spent the night with him if she had agreed to marry someone else. But James's words had felt like truth, and Trevor had never specifically asked Jennie about her status. He had just assumed she wasn't attached to anyone, since he hadn't detected a male scent on her.

Could he really have been that wrong about her? And why hadn't she had sex with Michael if she was going to marry him? Jennie certainly wasn't the religious type, and it wasn't like she was saving herself.

She had even mentioned that she was divorced. There didn't seem to be a logical reason for not having sex with the man she loved.

Jennie loved someone else. The pain in Trevor's chest startled him. It was obviously just the sting of betrayal, but it took him by surprise how much it hurt.

Perhaps it was for the best that this was how things ended between them. It was only a few days until she was leaving, anyway, and although he would have liked to spend a few more nights with her, he was already growing too attached as it was. It was time for him to move on and find a nice alpha female to mate. The thought did nothing to improve his mood. If possible, it seemed to deteriorate even further.

One thing he truly didn't understand was why she was going to marry Michael of all people. They didn't seem like a good match. Not at all.

Duncan's words came back to him all of a sudden. Trevor was sure it was Michael who had intentionally placed himself in Jennie's path, causing her to tip her kayak. But why would he do that if he cared about her?

An image appeared in his head of Jennie's astonished look when he kissed her knuckles before leaving her at the airport. Her friends had all witnessed his actions, and for all he knew, his admiration for Jennie might have been evident on his face at that moment. If Michael was anything like most shifters, it would have made him furious and crazy with jealousy. Trevor had seen it happen before with soon-to-be mated pairs. But why leave his soon-to-be mate behind in the baggage hall to fend for herself? It wasn't normal shifter behavior. And where was the affection between Jennie and Michael?

Jennie might not know how things worked in the shifter world, since she didn't even know their kind existed. But the affection between a couple that was going to be mated was usually unmistakable. The few times Trevor had been in the presence of both Jennie and Michael, he hadn't even been able to pick up that they were a couple.

Could it be possible that Jennie had agreed to marry Michael out of convenience? That didn't fit with Trevor's impression of Jennie, but which other possibilities were there? There didn't seem to be any real affection or apparent attachment between them.

One thing was for sure, though; Trevor needed to get away. There wasn't going to be any more nights with Jennie, and he didn't think he would be able to come face to face with her again without asking her why she had come to his bed when she was engaged to another man. Perhaps he was a coward for running and not confronting her about her behavior, but Trevor was sure that talking to her would reveal how betrayed he felt. And ultimately she hadn't promised him anything other than a few nights of pleasure.

"Fuck!" He hit the steering wheel hard, almost breaking the damn thing. *What a fucking mess.* But it served him right for letting his cock rule his actions. He should have stayed away from Jennie like he had kept telling himself from the beginning.

ooooo

It was late afternoon by the time they arrived back at the cottage. James and Carlos came out the front door as they were approaching and lovingly greeted their wives. Jennie used the opportunity to change direction toward her room, in order to unpack her shopping bags. As she rounded the corner of the cottage, Michael rose from the picnic table and approached her.

"I've been waiting for you," he said, giving her a self-confident smile.

Jennie didn't know what to say. She had thought she would be able to get to her room without speaking to him, but obviously she had been too hasty in drawing that conclusion.

"We need to talk," he continued, and without waiting for a response from her, Michael put his hand on the small of her back and pushed her toward the picnic table.

Jennie automatically took a few steps forward to avoid falling on her face. She turned toward Michael to tell him off, only to have his lips press against hers, startling her so much that she froze.

A few seconds went by before she felt his tongue lick at the seam of her lips. The feeling returned her ability to move, and she quickly snapped her head back at the same time as her hand came up and connected with his cheek with a sharp crack.

"How dare you!" Jennie's voice came out low and furious. "If you ever do that again, I'll knock your teeth out."

Michael glared at her. One hand came up to rub his red cheek while his other arm was tightly wrapped around her waist. "You're going to be my wife. Even if you're not in love with me, we're going to be intimate. If you just let me show you what I can give you in bed, there's no way you'll pass up this chance of a lifetime."

She tried to get out of his hold on her, but his arm was like a vice, holding her tightly pressed against him, seemingly without any effort at all.

"Michael, stop! Before I scream." Jennie strained to make a gap between their bodies while staring angrily into his eyes. He was starting to scare her, but she used her anger to hold off her fear.

She was just opening her mouth to scream, when Michael abruptly let her go and took two steps back. "I'm sorry." He looked away from her, deliberately not meeting her furious stare.

"You're an asshole!" Jennie's rage got the better of her, and she couldn't stop the tide of angry words pouring out. "I wouldn't marry you if you were the last man on this planet. I'd rather die a lonely old spinster than share your bed. No amount of money will ever be enough for you to buy me like some whore. And how dare you even suggest such a thing. I hate you!"

Jennie abruptly turned around and strode to her door. Her previous fear had evaporated with the eruption of her fury. Without looking back to check if Michael was following her, she calmly unlocked her door, entered, and slammed the door behind her.

As seconds turned into minutes, Jennie stood right inside the door, staring with unseeing eyes at the back wall of the room. Thoughts were racing through her brain in a big, confused mass, and she struggled to make sense of what had just happened.

Disbelief that Michael could sink so low as to try to force himself on her was warring with resentment toward her friends for inviting Michael to go on this trip. How could they possibly think she would want to go out with someone like him after what Olivier did to her? It was hard to accept that Ann and Marna didn't know how arrogant and vile Michael really was. But even if they didn't, their husbands had to know.

"Breathe," she told herself. "Just breathe."

What was she going to do? Staying in the same house as Michael had just become impossible. Jennie didn't trust him anymore. There was no telling what he would do next, since he obviously didn't understand that she really wanted nothing to do with him. He had set his mind on having her and wasn't going to back down no matter what she said. Her opinion of him and the fact that she told him no, had no effect on his effort to pursue her. On the contrary, it seemed to spur him on and make him more persistent.

There was really just one thing left to do.

∞∞∞

Michael's cheek stung as he made his way to his bedroom, carefully avoiding the couples in the kitchen. Ann and Marna were happily showing off all the stuff they had bought to their husbands, so it wasn't difficult to escape their attention.

He closed the door behind him silently and sat down on the bed. "Well, that sure as fuck didn't go as planned," he told himself quietly.

Closing his eyes, he lay back on the bed. Michael had no idea what to do to make amends with Jennie. He had royally fucked up, and telling her he was sorry wasn't going to be enough to make her forget that he had basically forced himself on her.

How could he have been so stupid? It might have worked and perhaps even been expected by some women but not Jennie. She wasn't some loose woman with no will of her own, letting guys call the shots for her. She didn't need a man to take care of her and make decisions for her. Jennie was perfectly capable of doing that for herself, and she expected the man in her life to respect and appreciate that.

Suddenly it was all so perfectly clear. Why hadn't he realized it before? Because he was desperate to secure himself a wife of his own choosing, instead of having one chosen for him. That was why. And it had cost him his chance with Jennie, the woman he wanted.

An image of Stephanie suddenly filled his mind. The memory of how she had felt in his arms as he carried her down the hill had him suck in a breath and snap his eyes open.

Michael sat up and shook his head as if to dislodge the memory. What was wrong with him? He had enough on his plate already. There was no room for this emotional crap. And about a timid little mouse no less. She would be eaten alive if she ever met his family. He needed a woman with a backbone, and Jennie was the perfect choice.

Well, he would never have thought that he would ever sink this low, but the time had come for begging. It was time to beg Jennie for her forgiveness and show her he could be everything she wanted. If she wanted a man who supported her as an author, he would do that. And if she wanted a husband who let her decide what they were going to do and when, he would do that with a smile on his face. As long as she accepted him and mated him, he would do and be anything she chose. It would be worth it. A sense of defeat settled into him, but he ignored it, telling himself it was all going to work out for the best.

CHAPTER 19

Ann, Marna, and their husbands were gathered around the kitchen table when Jennie entered the room. They looked so happy that for a second, she contemplated not going ahead with her plan. But only for a second. She really didn't have a choice.

"I'm so sorry to dampen your spirits." Jennie looked from one to the other of her two best friends and saw confusion in their eyes. "But I can't stay in the same house as Michael anymore."

Ann narrowed her eyes. "What has he done now?"

James put his hand on his wife's arm and looked at Jennie. "It's probably better if you talk to Michael about this. I'm sure it's something you can sort out if you just sit down and talk it through. That's what we do." He looked fondly at Ann.

Jennie felt her anger rising again. James made it sound like she and Michael were a couple. "No. I've spent enough time talking. He doesn't understand a word I'm saying. And I'm—"

"I'm sorry. For everything."

Michael's voice startled her, and she turned to see he had entered the kitchen and stood by the wall, looking at her with a sincere, almost sad, expression on his face.

It did nothing to temper her anger, though. "I don't trust you. Your words mean nothing. You say whatever you think will get you what you want. And you do whatever you feel like without any regard for other people's feelings. You're not sorry. I don't even think you know what that word means."

Michael nodded and didn't look away from her. "You're right. That's how I've been acting. I realize that now. And I am truly sorry, even if you don't think I know what that means."

James's chair scraping along the floor as he rose had Jennie looking at him. "I think you should talk about this in private. I'm sure there are details in your disagreement that we don't need to know about."

Jennie couldn't help snorting. "Why? It's not like he's my boyfriend or anything."

The frown on James's face had her looking at the others around the table. Ann and Marna didn't seem surprised by her statement, but Carlos did.

Jennie turned back to James and narrowed her eyes. "Why do I get the feeling that you thought there was something going on between Michael and me? Ann and Marna both know there isn't and never will be."

James moved his gaze from her to stare at Michael. His expression was unreadable when he spoke. "Michael, what's this about?"

There was definitely something going on that she didn't know about. Jennie didn't say anything, just turned to look at Michael.

There seemed to be some kind of power play going on. Michael was staring at the floor, clearly avoiding James's steady gaze. It was strange seeing the usually confident and arrogant man letting someone else have the upper hand and not even trying to stand up for himself. An image of James, Carlos, and Michael facing the three bikers at the beach popped into her head. James a little ahead of the other two like he was their leader, and Michael and Carlos accepting this like it was the natural order of things.

"I was sure she was going to accept me." Michael kept his eyes glued to the floor. "It was only a matter of time."

"You led me to believe she already had."

James's voice sounded angry, and the room felt a bit hot and stuffy all of a sudden. Jennie got the sudden urge to leave, but then the meaning of James's words sank in. Michael had told James that she had agreed to marry him. Not only had he been an ass to her and tried to force himself on her, but he had lied to his friends. If this didn't let the others understand what an asshole Michael was, nothing would.

Michael had yet to respond to James's statement, and Jennie decided this was as good a time as any for her to leave.

"Okay, I'm going to stay at Trevor's tonight," she said as she turned around to head back to her room to pack a few things.

A hand firmly gripping her upper arm made her stop and turn her head to see who was preventing her from leaving.

"Please don't leave. I'm sorry. I'll do anything to

make it up to you." Michael was staring at her, and if she didn't know better, she would have called his look pleading.

Anger boiled up inside her, and she barely stopped herself from hitting him. "Get. Your. Hand. Off. Me. *Now!*"

He released her arm, and she turned to face him. "You will never touch me again. Ever. I decide who's allowed to touch me. Not you. I'm going to stay at Trevor's tonight, like I have the last few nights."

Michael took a step back with a look of horror on his face. "You let the wolf fuck you?"

The gasp she heard from her friends at his outburst had her looking around at their faces. Ann and Marna were staring at her, and their expressions were a mixture of apprehension and fear. Which was odd since they already knew she'd had sex with Trevor. Were they worried how Jennie was going to react to Michael's disrespect? Well, she had nothing to be ashamed of. She had chosen to have sex with Trevor, and she was proud of herself for taking what she wanted for once.

Jennie let images of Trevor and what they had done together, in and out of bed, fill her mind, and her lips pulled up into a smile. "Yeah, and he's really good at it."

Before anyone could stop her, she turned around and hurried out the door. Once in her room, she grabbed her small backpack and stuffed her laptop, some clothes, and toiletries into it before locking the door to her room behind her and heading down the path toward the sea loch. It was still a couple of hours until she was supposed to meet Trevor, but she hoped he wouldn't mind her showing up at his place a bit early. He had seemed eager to see her again this evening, though, so she wasn't really that worried.

ooooo

Loch Ness finally came into view, and Trevor turned off the main road onto a smaller road following the east side of the loch. After just a few minutes, he pulled off the road and parked in front of a house beautifully situated in between the trees close to the water's edge.

He turned off the engine and just sat there for a little while. His anger had slowly given way to pain as he drove, but he didn't want to dwell on the fact that it felt like someone had ripped his heart from his chest and replaced it with a burning lump of coal.

"Suck it up, you idiot," he mumbled. "She hurt your pride. Deal with it. She's not the only woman in the world." Trevor opened the door and stepped out of the car. He sighed. If only he could make himself believe that, but at the moment he couldn't seem to see past Jennie to a life without her. It just felt wrong.

"It has been a long time, my friend." The deep voice belonged to a man with a tall and lean yet strong body.

"It has, Leith."

They grasped each other's forearms in a firm hold for several seconds before letting go.

Leith's broody expression seldom changed, and Trevor had rarely heard the man laugh, but he was a good man and never one to shy away from helping others. They had known each other for years, and

Trevor always knew he could rely on his friend to give him his fair opinion. Usually after taking his time assessing the issue carefully.

"You look like you have been to hell and back, my friend. Is that why you are here? How can I help?"

Leith had a tendency to read people's expressions and body language like an open book, and it made keeping anything secret from the man virtually impossible. Not that Trevor usually had something to hide. Leith could be trusted, and Trevor didn't feel any need to keep things from his friend.

"I don't think you'd be able to help me with this, but if you don't mind me staying for a few days, it would be greatly appreciated." Trevor was surprised at the resignation in his own voice. He sounded like he'd lost an important battle.

"Ah, a woman." Leith frowned. "Not like you to run away from a challenge. Is she not worth fighting for?"

Trevor was a bit taken aback at Leith's words. It really made him sound like a coward. And he wasn't running away. He was just getting out of the way because he didn't want to interfere with Jennie's engagement to another man. Which actually sounded a lot like running away instead of fighting when he thought about it.

"Jennie would be worth fighting for, but she's not for me. I need to mate an alpha female, and she's not even a wolf. Even if I won her, I couldn't keep her. It's better this way."

Leith studied him for what felt like a long time while considering what he had said. Then he turned and headed toward the house. "Come, my friend. I think there are a few beers waiting for us in the fridge."

ꝏꝏꝏ

Jennie looked around carefully before opening the gate to Trevor's big lawn. His dog didn't seem to be around, but she opened the gate slowly and made sure to step on a twig to announce her arrival as she took a couple of tentative steps into the garden. She could still escape back out through the gate and slam it closed if the dog appeared.

After waiting a full minute without any sign of the big canine, she closed the gate behind her and made her way slowly to the back door of Trevor's house.

Jennie knocked and waited for what felt like a long time. Maybe he wasn't home. It was still quite a while until they were supposed to meet, so he was probably out tending to his animals or something.

She was just preparing to settle in to wait on the steps when the door opened, and Duncan stared at her like she had been lost at sea for a year and presumed dead.

"Um, is Trevor home?" Jennie felt awkward for asking. She obviously wasn't welcome. Perhaps it was a bad time. It wasn't like they were seeing each other or anything. She should have just gone for a walk and returned to wait at the usual place by the sea loch at ten thirty. Jennie had just been so sure Trevor would be happy to see her.

"I don't think you should be here." The anger in Duncan's voice hit her like a fist to her stomach, and she took a step back. "You should've been straight with him. At least then he would've known what to expect."

Jennie didn't know what to say. She wasn't sure what Duncan was talking about, but it was obvious he didn't think she had been honest with Trevor. Only she couldn't figure out what had made him think so.

"He's gone, and if he knows what's best for him, he'll stay away until you've left."

Jennie gasped as the knife tore into her heart. Not a literal knife, of course, but that was how it felt. She stumbled back another step and would have fallen on her ass if she hadn't managed to grab ahold of...Duncan. He had moved so fast she hadn't even seen it.

"Are you all right?" The anger in his voice from before had been replaced by concern.

Jennie couldn't help the hysterical laughter that erupted as her heart bled and slowly died in her chest. "Yeah, why wouldn't I be? I'll just be on my way now."

Trying to focus, she attempted to turn around and start walking, but it was like her body wasn't hers to command anymore. She felt so tired, like she hadn't slept for days. And what was the point, anyway? She had nowhere to go. Tears were threatening to escape, and her vision started to blur.

No, this wasn't her. She was stronger than this. At least if she was going to have a breakdown, it wasn't going to be there. Jennie forced her legs to move and pulled out of Duncan's hold on her. Taking one sluggish step at a time, she slowly made her way back to the garden gate and back down the way she had come. There was no way she was going to go back to the cottage, but she would find somewhere to stay the night, even if that meant staying outside.

***

Duncan watched Jennie walk away, her movements stiff and staccato. He couldn't shake the feeling that he had just watched her die. Her body was still alive, but something inside her had seemed to shatter.

Was it possible that she really cared about Trevor? But how could that be when she was going to mate someone else? It just didn't make any sense. Shifters weren't like that. But then she wasn't a shifter, was she? She was human, so anything was possible.

Most likely he had just witnessed her reaction to finding out her plan had failed. It must be a shock to realize the truth was out, and that Trevor was gone and no longer hers to play with.

Fuck, what a mess. Duncan had actually started believing that Trevor had found his mate, and he had been ready to accept Jennie as one of the humans who knew about their kind. Duncan had been happy for Trevor. A mate would be good for his friend, and any resulting pups would liven up the place.

Duncan couldn't see himself ever finding a mate and settling down. That kind of life wasn't for him. But being an uncle, if only through friendship, would be fun. And he would happily teach them anything they needed to know about being a wolf.

He sighed and went back inside the house. Perhaps Trevor would find himself a nice alpha female. Although that was often a bit of a contradiction, as female alpha wolves tended to be bitches in the worst sense of the word. They were usually so strong-willed and arrogant that they tended to drive their men a bit crazy.

ꝏꝏꝏ

Trevor felt Leith's eyes on him as they sat across from each other at the kitchen table in Leith's house. The kitchen, like the rest of the house, looked like it could belong in a museum. There were ancient artifacts on the mantel above the huge old hearth and scenic, old paintings on the walls, and every wooden beam in the ceiling was carved into intricate shapes and patterns. And still with all this artwork, the room felt warm and welcoming.

"Whenever you are ready, my friend." Leith's voice broke the long silence between them.

Trevor sighed and set down his beer. "Jennie fell into my arms. Literally, on the plane over here. And she's been stuck in my head ever since. If she and her friends hadn't rented a cottage in Fearolc to stay, I might've been able to forget about her, but as it turned out, they had. I should've stayed away, but she's like a magnet, and I wasn't able to wait more than a couple of hours before I sought her out."

Trevor turned his head and met Leith's gaze. "She's beautiful, of course, but Jennie's so much more than that. I don't think I've ever met anyone like her. She's strong yet kind and considerate, not hesitating to put others welfare ahead of her own. And she's warm and passionate."

Leith had raised one corner of his mouth a little, in what was usually his version of a smile. "From the look on your face, I would say you have had firsthand experience with her passionate side." It wasn't a question.

Trevor chuckled. "Yes, that's putting it mildly. Hands, mouth, dick, and all. Two nights that will be hard to forget. I've never had a woman like her before."

"Why does it have to stop?" Leith's expression had changed back to the broody one again.

Sighing, Trevor looked at his friend. "I found out that she's to be mated to another shifter.

Leith's eyebrows raised a fraction. "Willingly?"

"Yes." Trevor frowned. "I'm quite sure, yes. That's what I was told, and the man's words felt like truth to me. I usually can tell when someone is lying to me."

Leith didn't say anything, just inclined his head to indicate that Trevor should continue.

Trevor studied the label on his beer bottle before lifting it to his mouth and downing the rest of its contents. It was a good beer and deserved to be enjoyed slowly, but nothing tasted well at the moment.

"I don't know if there's much more to tell. That's it really."

Leith narrowed his eyes at him. "So, you are fine with letting that be the end of it? What did she say when you confronted her with what you had learned?"

Trevor didn't meet Leith's eyes. "I didn't. I jumped in the car, just wanting to get out of there." He lifted his gaze to Leith's. "I know it seems like I ran away, but what's the point? She's to be mated to some kind of cat shifter, and it's just better for everyone if I stay out of it. And besides, she's human. Mating Jennie would be wrong. I'm expected to mate an alpha female. I'd have to give her up at some stage, anyway, to find a mate, so it's for the best that this happened now before I could grow attached to her."

Leith's snort had Trevor raising his eyebrows in surprise. It was a sound he'd hardly ever heard his friend make.

Then Leith shook his head slowly, and Trevor frowned in confusion. Something was up with his friend, but he had no idea what it was.

"You have not taken time to think this through, have you?" Leith was looking at him intently. "I have never heard you utter a woman's name when speaking about mating. Until now mating has been an event far into the future for you, and something you have spoken of with distaste. But when you speak of not being able to mate Jennie, it is with regret in your voice. I never thought I would ever say these words to you, but you are wrong, my friend. You are running because you are afraid of your attraction to her, and you are afraid of being hurt when confronting her about her apparent deception. But why be afraid of being hurt when you are already in pain? The only certain way to lose her is to give up fighting for what you truly want. And in case you have not realized it yet, what you want is Jennie, with all your heart."

Trevor heard the words, but the meaning was just outside his grasp. His mind was struggling to make sense of what Leith was saying, and he could only sit there staring at his friend while his mind was busy solving the riddle.

"I am going for a swim." Leith got up and moved toward the door. "My mind is working better when I am in the water. Perhaps I will think of a way to help you."

Trevor wasn't capable of speech yet. His mind was

a jumble of words, and the two most prevalent ones were Jennie and mate. But that couldn't be. She couldn't be. Jennie was human.

Images from the last few days spun through his head. Jennie on the plane. Her heart-stopping smile before she returned to her seat. The feel of her body against his as she hugged him after he returned her purse in the airport. Her naked body on his bed with her head flung back, as the climax he had given her rode her body. His dick grew rock hard just thinking about it. Trevor had wanted to mark her right there and then. The urge had been strong. He'd never felt anything like it before. Could Leith actually be right? Duncan had even asked him whether he was sure that Jennie wasn't his mate.

Trevor shook his head to try to clear it and make sense of all his thoughts and feelings. All he knew was that he'd never been hurt by a woman before. They came and went from time to time, and there had been both humans and shifters. But none of them had ever made a lasting impression on him. Until Jennie.

She had made him forget everything else but her. When he was with her, there was no tomorrow, no other people, no concerns or worries. There was only her and what he could do for her, to her. All he wanted was to make sure she had everything she desired.

He suddenly felt warm, and his heart started racing. Was Jennie really his mate? He didn't know the answer to that question, but just the possibility put a huge grin on his face.

CHAPTER 20

Michael sat on the edge of his bed, staring at the floor. James had been really pissed off with him after Jennie left, and Carlos had to intervene to prevent James from laying into him. Understandable, since Michael had intentionally led them to believe that Jennie had agreed to marry him. James was his friend and not Michael's alpha, but he was still a powerful alpha and as such demanded respect.

James had needed a timeout to calm down, and Michael had retreated to his bedroom for a while to allow his friend some time and space to settle. It was only a matter of time before he would be asked to explain himself; he knew that. And he was currently debating what to say.

He had to tell the truth. The question was rather what he could or should leave out. James would be able to tell if Michael downright lied to him. His friends had believed Jennie had agreed to marry Michael only because Michael had carefully phrased his recount of the proposal in such a way that the logical assumption was that Jennie had said *yes*. And of course, Michael had done nothing to prevent James and Carlos from making that assumption.

His anger spiked as he recalled what Jennie had said about spending the last few nights with the wolf. If Michael had been paying better attention, he would have realized what was going on. It was there in her scent. A subtle change, but it was there. But the truth was that he had ignored it because he thought he must be mistaken. Jennie was better than that. If anything, she seemed to be a bit of a prude, and Michael had never expected her to sneak off at night to fuck the asshole without him noticing. He had been played for a fool. Well, not really, since she had never promised him anything. But that was how it felt.

"Michael, would you mind joining us in the kitchen please?" Ann's voice outside his bedroom door had him standing up.

"I'm coming." Michael straightened his shoulders and lifted his chin. James might be an alpha, but he wasn't Michael's boss.

They were all gathered around the kitchen table when he entered, and even though he could still feel James's power lingering in the room, it was tamped down significantly from earlier.

Michael picked the chair directly opposite James and sat down facing him. He forced himself to meet James's stare and sat there, calmly waiting for James to address him. There was no point opening the conversation to try to get a head start. Calm and collected conveyed more confidence and indicated he was open for this conversation and had nothing to hide.

"Why did you let me believe Jennie had agreed to marry you?" James's voice was carefully controlled, but Michael could feel the anger simmering below the surface.

Michael stuck to the truth. "Because I was hoping she'd say yes within a few days, when she had a chance to get used to the idea."

"You honestly believed that?"

Michael sighed. "As I said, I was hoping. Maybe I should've understood that the idea wasn't actually growing on her. Rather the opposite was true." He narrowed his eyes in anger but kept it tamped down to not aggravate James. "But I had no idea she was fucking the wolf, and that might've had something to do with her refusing me."

"To be honest I don't think you ever stood a chance with her." Ann obviously couldn't keep out of the conversation, and she kept talking, even though James put a hand firmly on her arm to indicate that she should leave this to him. "And the way you've been pushing her the last few days, I think it was only a matter of time before it would blow up in your face."

"Yes, I guess I've been pushing her quite hard to get her to accept me." There was no reason to deny it. "Jennie's so different from most of the women I know. They expect a man to be persistent if he really wants someone. It is a show of respect and desire. Anything less is a sign of indifference, and no woman wants that in her man."

James's stare softened, and he shook his head slowly. "I forget that you've grown up with an entirely different social code to what I'm used to. I should've taken that into account, and I'm sorry that I didn't. But please, next time try to meet me halfway. I will ask more questions to make sure I know the full story without jumping to conclusions, and you should give me more details from the start so I can get a clear view of the full picture."

Michael nodded. He had gotten off easy. "I'm sorry."

James frowned. "How do you feel, though, now that you know Jennie's not going to accept you?"

He shrugged and looked away. "I don't know." Michael didn't want to tell them that this left him with a problem. He wouldn't be surprised if his father already had a woman waiting at home for him when he got back. And if Michael couldn't convince his old man that he was already engaged to someone else, he would be married to his father's choice of woman for him within a few weeks.

"If you'd excuse me, I think I'll go for a walk." Michael pushed the chair back and stood.

"Of course." James got up as well. "Please tell us if there's anything we can do for you."

"Thank you."

Michael stepped out of the cottage and headed down toward the water. He had no idea what to do. All he could think about was what awaited him when he got back home, and how much he didn't want that. There had to be some way to avoid the forced mating his father intended for him.

∞∞∞

Jennie wasn't sure how long she had been walking,

or where she was for that matter. She hadn't been paying attention. The pain in her chest was so severe it had taken over completely for a while. She was just realizing that hours must have gone by since she left Trevor's house, and it was getting dark. It wouldn't be long before she would have trouble finding her way in the dark.

She gasped as pain radiated out from her chest again, where it felt like a knife twisted in her heart. Tears were blurring her vision, and she let them flow. There was no reason to stop them.

Jennie had understood that she was falling for Trevor, and she had expected it to be hard to leave him at the end of the week. But she had never anticipated their fling ending like this and the pain being so extreme.

She sat down on a rock and just breathed. How was she going to cope, knowing it ended so badly? From the way Duncan had reacted at seeing her, Trevor had been hurt by something she did. But what? She didn't have the faintest idea what it could be, and asking Duncan to elaborate didn't seem like a good plan. He was angry because Jennie had hurt his friend, even though she didn't know how.

There were mountains surrounding her on all sides, and Jennie wasn't sure which direction she had come from. It was pretty clear she wasn't going to find her way back in the dark, so she would have to find a place to sleep somewhere close by.

Looking around, she decided to try to find shelter within the trees by the hillside behind her. It seemed like the best option, since she didn't want to sleep out in the open.

After about twenty minutes of making her way slowly through the dense, almost impenetrable thicket, she found three big boulders leaning toward each other and forming a small shelter. She just managed to squeeze through the opening, crawling on her belly.

It wasn't exactly comfortable in the small space in between the boulders, but it was reasonably dry, and after putting on all the extra clothes she had stuffed into her backpack, it was warm enough.

Jennie tried to find a comfortable position so she could get some rest until it got light enough for her to find her way back to Fearolc. She had no hope of falling asleep after everything that had happened that day, but at least her body would get some rest.

∞∞∞

Trevor was still sitting at the kitchen table when Leith walked into the room. His long copper-colored hair was still dripping, and he pulled a towel off a hook by the hearth and put it around his hair in an elaborate twist somewhat like a turban.

Trevor chuckled. "This is the first time I've seen a man curl a towel around his hair like that."

Leith shrugged and went over to the coffee maker. "Well, there is a first time for everything. And besides, I am man enough to carry it off."

Trevor laughed. "In your own house. Sure."

"Says the man who just ran away instead of fighting for the woman he wants." Leith raised an eyebrow at him.

"That's low." Trevor scowled.

"But true, my friend." Leith brought two cups of

coffee to the table and put one in front of Trevor. "And you have to go back and fight for her before it is too late. I have no doubt that she is your mate, and your future happiness depends on claiming her for your own. If I ever find my mate, I will claim her in a heartbeat."

"But how can you be so sure that she's my mate? I'm not even sure."

One side of Leith's mouth lifted slightly. "Ah, but the idea of having her by your side and in your bed for the rest of your life does not feel bad to you, does it?"

The idea of Jennie in his bed had his cock thickening. "Well no, but—"

"Exactly!" Leith stared at him like he had just given the final indisputable proof in court and won his case.

Trevor frowned. "That doesn't prove anything."

Leith sighed, and his expression reverted to his normal broody one. "Think of any one of the women you have courted, bedded, or both in your life. Can you imagine spending the rest of your life with one of them?"

The thought filled Trevor with such distaste that he felt like throwing up. "Of course not. There's a reason why I let them go. That still doesn't prove anything."

"Okay." Leith sipped his coffee. "Perhaps you are right. She might not be your mate, and in that case, I know someone who would happily take your mind off things. She lives just—"

"I don't want another woman!" Trevor realized he was standing, and the echo of his yelling was still audible throughout the house.

Leith looked at him with one eyebrow raised. "Now do you believe me?"

Trevor didn't know what to say. Just the thought of being with another woman made him feel ill. The only one he wanted was Jennie, in his bed and in his life, forever. The realization shocked him. Jennie was his mate.

ooooo

The sound of something moving through the trees, making strange noises, woke Jennie from her sleep. She lay completely still just listening, hoping that whatever animal was moving around out there would go away.

The light coming in through the cracks between the boulders was faint, indicating it was still quite dark and not yet morning.

The sounds outside seemed to spread, and Jennie realized it had to be more than one animal moving around. She wasn't normally scared of the dark or wild animals, but she suddenly felt extremely alone and exposed, even though she was well hidden within the safety of the boulders.

Very slowly and without making a sound she got up on her knees. There was just room enough to allow her to look through a narrow opening between the rocks close to the top of the space she was in.

At first all she could see were the trees. Something was still moving around out there, but not within the area that was visible to her through the opening. Then a shadow seemed to change right on the edge of her field of vision. She tried to angle her head to be able to get a better view, but she didn't have a lot of room to move.

Jennie hoped the animals hadn't caught her scent and were trying to get to her. There were no large carnivores in Scotland, but an angry Highland cow would be no less frightening or dangerous to meet. They wouldn't be able to get into the space where she was hidden, though, so she was safe.

After a couple of minutes, the sounds became fainter, and she sat down. The animals were obviously moving away.

It was still too dark for her to try to find her way back to the village, so Jennie lay down and tried to get comfortable. Even if she didn't fall asleep again at least she could rest for a while longer.

Thoughts of Trevor came unbidden, and she gasped as her already wounded heart seemed to tear open even more. The pain was worse than anything she had ever experienced before, and in response she curled up in a fetal position.

How could she have fallen for him so completely in just a few days? It shouldn't be possible. But if she didn't know better, she would think she actually loved him. She had never met anyone like him, and he easily outshone everyone around him. Jennie couldn't imagine ever meeting anyone like him again. She had no doubt that Trevor was it for her. There could be no one else, because no one would ever be able to measure up to him.

If only she knew how she had hurt him or pissed him off enough to leave, but she had absolutely no clue. The last time she saw Trevor, they were saying goodbye at the shore of the sea loch, and he had said he couldn't wait to see her again that night. So, what had happened after that? Had someone else said something about her? It had to be some kind of misunderstanding.

Jennie, Ann, and Marna had spent most of the day in Fort William, and nothing they had done in Fort William would have hurt Trevor in any way. The guys had been staying in Fearolc, but what could they possibly have done to make Trevor leave?

The whole confrontation between Michael and James suddenly came back to her. James had been convinced that she had accepted Michael's proposal of marriage, and he had been really angry with Michael when it turned out not to be true. Was it possible that James had met Trevor during the day and told him that Jennie was engaged to Michael? It was possible, but was it likely?

She thought of Michael's anger and jealousy toward Trevor, and suddenly everything became crystal clear in her mind. Michael. He was, of course, behind this. He had been jealous of Trevor from the first time he'd seen him in the airport, and Michael wanted to make sure she agreed to marry him. He had no doubt noticed her attraction to Trevor, and her staying the night at Trevor's house after the hiking trip in the mountains had only fueled his jealousy. Telling Trevor of their engagement was the perfect way to make sure Trevor stayed away from her.

No wonder Trevor had left. They had never promised each other anything other than a few nights of sex, but to find out that she was engaged must have felt wrong. Even if they weren't dating, it would still feel like a form of deception on her part. But why hadn't Trevor stayed and asked her about it? Wouldn't that have been the natural thing to do? But then he probably couldn't be bothered. It wasn't like she was important to him.

CHAPTER 21

Michael woke up with a start, drenched in sweat, his body stuck in the twisted sheets. Panting, he stared at the ceiling with unseeing eyes. Even though he knew he was awake, his mind was still stuck in the nightmare he had just woken from.

He had been standing, waiting at the altar with James and Carlos, waiting for his bride to walk up the aisle. When the church doors opened and she appeared, the sight of Jennie in her long, flowing wedding dress had him smiling. Pleased that he had won, he turned to his father, who was seated at the front. His father's evil grin had him take a step back in shock and look around to find out what was making his father so pleased.

Michael's eyes were drawn to the woman in a tight red dress standing on the second-floor gallery. She was staring at him, and her eyes were full of terror, like she was witnessing something horrible taking place. He looked around, but nothing out of the ordinary was going on.

Gazing back up at the woman, he noticed that she wasn't wearing a dress at all, but her skin was coated in blood like she had been swimming in it. And suddenly he recognized her face. It was Stephanie.

His father's maniacal laughter startled him, and his old man sneered with mad joy when Michael turned his head to look at him. "Serves you right, Son. Take the bride you have chosen and forget that gray mouse of a mate. She's too weak for you, anyway."

Michael untangled the sheets from around his legs and torso. What the hell was that about? He didn't usually dream, and he couldn't remember the last time he'd had a nightmare.

At least the dream didn't have any truth to it. He wasn't going to marry Jennie. That ship had well and truly sailed. And as for Stephanie, that she might be his mate was just crazy.

He kept wondering, though, how she had ended up hurt up in the hills all by herself. She had been terrified. But for some reason, he got the feeling that the fact that she could have died up there if they hadn't found her wasn't the source of her fear. She had held onto him like he was her hero. That was the reason he hadn't wanted anyone else to carry her down from the mountain.

Michael got out of bed and forced all lingering thoughts of the dream to the back of his mind. It was time to move on with his life. If he was going to secure himself a mate by the end of this trip, he needed a plan. There was no more time to waste. His father was not going to win.

ꝏꝏꝏ

It was light outside the next time Jennie woke up, but it was still really early in the morning. She was just about to sit up when she heard noises outside again. Sighing inwardly, she carefully sat up and squeezed into place to look outside through the narrow crack between the boulders.

What she saw sent a tremor through her body, and she just managed to stop herself from gasping. She didn't want to make any noises to attract the animals' attention.

There were two of them, one a bit darker gray than the other, and there was no doubt in her mind that these were wolves and not dogs. They looked almost identical to the wolf in the painting she had seen at the museum.

The big animals were about thirty yards away, and Jennie was sincerely hoping they weren't going to come any closer. They were standing still at the moment, carefully evaluating their surroundings. Perhaps an odd way to describe the behavior of animals, but that was how it appeared to her. They looked so intelligent standing there. No wonder people had made up stories of these creatures being partially human. It was totally understandable.

But there weren't supposed to be wolves in Scotland anymore. They had been extinct for centuries. Somebody had obviously made a mistake when coming to that conclusion. Or these wolves were bred by someone. It was possible these animals had been brought into this country and raised in captivity before they were released, or perhaps escaped, into the wild.

The wolves started moving again, slowly and silently walking toward where Jennie was hidden. She felt her whole body stiffen in fear; even her breathing seized in her chest. They had scented her, and they were coming for her. And there was nothing she could do about it. She would end her life as wolf food in the Scottish Highlands, and nobody would ever find her remains because there wouldn't be any remains to be found.

What happened next would forever alter her life. Jennie had no idea whether she made a sound or not. She might have or the utter shock that seemed to roll through her body like a wave might have prevented it.

The snout of the darker gray wolf seemed to shorten and retract into its face at the same time as its fur started to recede. The creature's body started shaking and distorting like something inside of it was trying to get out. Jennie felt nauseous and wanted to look away, but her body was like a statue rooted to the spot, not allowing her to move or close her eyes.

The transformation seemed to go on forever, but in reality it probably only took a few seconds. The body of the wolf changed into a tall, muscular man, standing buck naked in between the trees. He was handsome, and nothing about his human appearance was remotely "wolfish". Based on how he looked, there was no reason to suspect he was anything other than human.

"These mixed scents are confusing." The man was looking at the wolf beside him, clearly talking to it and not to Jennie. "But the deer scent is fresher than the human one, and I think maybe the human scent is older than it seems."

The other wolf started changing and Jennie wasn't able to look away this time either. But it was a mixture of fascination and horror that kept her eyes trained on the unexplainable event taking place right in front of her eyes.

In the second wolf's place stood a beautiful woman. Tall for a human woman with a strong, muscular yet feminine body. It answered the question of whether female werewolves existed. Not that Jennie had come so far as to ponder that question yet.

"I agree." The woman was looking around. "She's probably long gone by now. Just as well since its already light, and we'd be in a hell of lot of trouble if somebody saw us. We'd better head back before everyone gets up."

"Sure you don't want to linger for a while?" The man turned toward the woman and was looking at her with lust radiating off him. "We can practice our pup-making skills." His wicked grin was one of desire but also of love.

The smile on the woman's face reflected the man's desire and love, and she turned toward him and reached up to cup his face in her hands.

Jennie was both captivated and horrified. It was beautiful the love that obviously existed between these two people, or werewolves, but she didn't want to bear witness to them having sex. Even if she closed her eyes or sat down so she couldn't see them, she would still be able to hear them.

"Let's hurry back, my love." The woman let her arms fall to her sides. "We'd never be back before people start moving about if you touch me. You know I can't get enough of you, and we'd probably stay for hours."

The man sighed in frustration but smiled at his girlfriend, or whatever it was called with wolves. "You're right."

They both changed back into wolves, and within seconds they disappeared among the trees as they most likely headed home.

Jennie sat down slowly. Her body still felt a bit frozen from the shock of what she had just witnessed, and she still couldn't believe it had happened at all. Had she actually just seen wolves changing into people or had she started seeing things? Lack of food might have affected her brain. She hadn't eaten since the late lunch they had enjoyed in Fort William the day before, not counting Marna's sweets on the train back to Fearolc.

And the implications if what she had seen was true were staggering. One thing was the actual existence of werewolves, which was a massive revelation in itself. But the bigger question was what else was out there? How many other species existed that the world, at least most of the human world, didn't know about? And how did they manage to stay hidden?

Then again, people tended to see what they expected to see, and anything that didn't fit their notion of normal was somehow explained as a variation of a known phenomenon or just labeled as a plain-old hallucination. Nothing extraordinary about it, see?

But Jennie knew what she had just experienced was real. Werewolves existed and probably a lot of other mythical creatures did as well. Which meant that the world was far more complicated and fantastic than she had ever imagined, but also more terrifying and mysterious. She had no idea how to handle this new knowledge yet, how to deal with what she had discovered. What was she going to tell her friends?

Her friends. It felt like an icy hand was moving its fingers down her spine, and she shivered. Her friends already knew. She was sure of it. Somehow they knew, but they hadn't wanted to tell her. Why was that, when they had shared so much through the years?

The confrontation with the bikers on the beach came back to her, and it was like her memory shifted and took on new meaning. The men weren't part of a motorcycle club. They were werewolves living in this area, their territory as they called it. And they had been pissed off with her friends for staying within their territory, but Jennie had been welcome to stay. Which could only mean that her friends were werewolves as well, but not belonging to this territory. Or maybe not. The men had called this wolf country like her friends were something else. Did that mean that her friends were some other kind of wereanimal?

Jennie shook her head to clear it. This was a lot to take in, and it would probably take her a while to digest everything. But she didn't really have time to do that. As soon as she found her way back to Fearolc, the name suddenly totally appropriate, she would have to confront her friends with her new knowledge. There was no way around it. This was bigger than her being angry with Michael and not wanting to stay in the same house as him. Thank God she wasn't attracted to him, or she might have ended up the wife of one of these creatures without even knowing it.

CHAPTER 22

Trevor had debated whether to go directly to the Miller's cottage where Jennie was staying or check in with Duncan first. Time was of the essence in securing Jennie as his mate before the cat managed to convince her to mate with him. But the more he had been thinking about it, Trevor felt sure that Jennie was holding Michael off. Even though she had agreed to marry the guy, they hadn't had sex, and knowing how passionate a person Jennie was, that had to mean she was stalling.

So, either the mating happened last night, which would mean Trevor was fucked, or her friends were taking their time preparing her for the revelation of the shifter world. And he was betting on the latter being the case. That might even be what this trip was all about, to break her in easy, so to speak.

He parked the car outside and entered his house through the front door. Duncan was in the kitchen when he entered, and he seemed a bit surprised to see him.

"Back already?" Duncan lifted an eyebrow at him. "I thought you were going to stay away at least until she left."

Trevor grinned. "Change of plans. Turns out Jennie's my mate. Do you remember asking me about that? Well, you were right."

Duncan going pale had Trevor frowning, and his heart rate sped up.

"What's wrong?" Trevor stared at Duncan.

"Jennie."

Duncan paused and Trevor lost it, stalking over to him and grabbing his upper arms. All his thoughts narrowed down to one. "What's wrong with Jennie?" His alpha power sent a shockwave through the house like a small earthquake, but he didn't even notice it.

"She came by after you left yesterday evening, asking for you. I told her you were gone, and that she should've told you." Duncan shook his head slowly. "It seemed to hurt her, but I thought she was probably just sorry that she wouldn't have you to play with anymore. But if Jennie's your mate, and she thought she'd lost you—"

"*No!*" The sound of anguish in his own voice seemed to wake Trevor from the trancelike state he was in.

He released his grip on Duncan, took a deep breath, and started pacing. "But she's not a wolf. There's no reason she would act like one." Because the implications of that were too horrible to consider. A wolf denied its mate was prone to sink into a despair so deep it often ended up taking its own life.

Trevor spun to face Duncan. "Where did she go?"

Duncan shrugged. "I assume back to her friends. Where else would she go?"

"Good point." Trevor started toward the back door. "I need to talk to her."

He didn't bother taking the car. He would get there faster by running.

It only took him a few minutes to get to the Miller's cottage, and he ran right up to the door to Jennie's room where she was staying at the south end of the cottage. It was only seven thirty in the morning, but he needed to make sure she was all right. But even though he kept pounding on her door and yelling her name, there was no response.

"What the fuck are you doing?"

Trevor turned around to see James standing there in his boxers and nothing else. He had obviously just woken up, probably by Trevor's pounding on Jennie's door.

"Where's Jennie?" The sudden realization that she might have spent the night in Michael's bed had Trevor's anger spiking.

But James's response wasn't the one Trevor had expected.

"Isn't she with you? She said she was going to stay at your place." James was frowning at him and seemed genuinely confused.

Trevor felt fear rising in him and gripping his spine, sending tendrils of icy needles all the way out to his extremities. "No, she's not. When did she leave?"

"Yesterday, around eight in the evening. She was really pissed off with Michael and said she didn't want to stay in the same house as him anymore. And I'm sorry, by the way. Michael led me to believe that Jennie had agreed to marry him when, in fact, she hadn't. She was furious when she found out that we all believed they were engaged. Or at least Carlos and I believed they were. Our wives knew better, apparently."

"So, you haven't seen her after she left last night?" Trevor was struggling to keep his fear from progressing into full-blown panic. He had never been this scared in his life.

James shook his head. "No. As I said, we believed she was with you. There was no reason for us to be concerned about her. According to my wife, Jennie really likes you."

Trevor closed his eyes and tried to get a grip on his emotions. Jennie needed him. He had to find her. And the cats could help him do that.

He opened his eyes and stared at James, letting his concern and fear fill his eyes. "Jennie's my mate, and I've fucked up. She might be in danger because of me. Please help me find her."

Astonishment and concern played over James's face. "What have you done?"

"After you came to my house yesterday, I left and stayed at a friend's house. I was angry and hurt, and determined not to come back until after you guys left Fearolc."

James narrowed his eyes at him. "You went to see another woman?"

"No! Fuck no!" Trevor threw his hands in the air in agitation. "I'd rather eat my tail."

"Then what?" James looked confused.

"Duncan said Jennie came by my house, looking for me yesterday evening, and he told her I was gone. She was hurt and left. But if she didn't come back here, then where the hell did she go? Wolf mates who are denied their true mates sometimes fall into a despair so deep they…" Trevor couldn't say the words. He just couldn't face that possibility. "And it must've been clear to her yesterday that I didn't want anything more to do with her. She's human, and she doesn't know that I'm a wolf and that she's my mate. Hell, I didn't even understand that she's my mate until late last night. But even though she's not a wolf, my denying her might've affected her somehow. I don't know. I just don't know. Please help me find her. I beg you." Trevor couldn't remember ever having begged for anything before, but for Jennie he'd crawl on his knees, kissing the dirt if that would bring her back to him.

"Of course." James's expression had turned progressively more concerned as Trevor had been talking. "Jennie's like family to me. She's one of my wife's best friends and practically like my sister. We'll do everything we can to help you find her. Fuck, my wife's going to have my hide if something has happened to Jennie. This is all my fault for not making sure I knew the truth before warning you to stay away from her."

"No." Trevor shook his head firmly. "I should've stayed and fought for her. This is all on me."

"I'll wake the others." James disappeared around the corner of the cottage.

Trevor looked at the locked door to Jennie's room. There was only one thing to do. The whole structure shook as the door splintered.

The bed was made with a few pieces of clothing strewn across it, and scenting her sheets confirmed that Jennie hadn't been sleeping in her bed. She probably hadn't been back there at all since she left for his house last night.

Looking around, he established that most of her clothes were still in the room. She hadn't brought a lot with her, probably just enough to stay at his place for the night. Even her phone was still there. He groaned. How could he have been such an idiot and not understood that Jennie was special? No other woman had ever made him feel the way she did, and still he had dismissed the idea of her being his mate. The truth was that he didn't deserve her. She was too good for him.

He extracted his phone from his pocket and called Duncan.

Duncan answered on the first ring. "Is she all right?"

"She's not here. Her friends haven't seen her since she left for my house yesterday evening. You're the last person to see her. In which direction did she go when she left my house?"

"Back toward the Miller's cottage like I told you. That's why I assumed she'd gone back to her friends." Duncan sighed. "But there's no telling where she might've headed if she didn't go back to the cottage. Do you want me to ask around if someone has seen her?"

Trevor nodded but realized Duncan couldn't see what he was doing. "Yes, that would be great. If we knew which direction she headed, it would narrow down our search. The cats will help me look for her."

"I'll call you if I find out anything useful." Duncan hung up.

ooooo

Michael returned from his early morning walk to find everyone up and an atmosphere of anger and fear so strong it threatened to choke him. Whatever had happened while he was gone wasn't good.

He stopped dead on seeing Trevor rounding the corner of the cottage and remained standing there, waiting for the wolf to notice him. Realization sank into his brain. That was why everyone was so agitated. The wolf was there to get revenge for what he had done to Jennie.

The moment Trevor saw him it was like the air filled with electricity. The alpha power rolling off the wolf was so commanding Michael had to fight to remain on his feet. His knees were shaking, and the urge to kneel was almost unbearable even though he wasn't a wolf.

Trevor's face was an unreadable mask as he stood a few yards away, staring at him. Michael had no doubt the wolf would be coming for him any second. And he also knew he wouldn't fight back. Whatever Trevor did to him, he deserved it for the way he had treated Jennie, and at least in this he would act like a real man and take what was coming to him.

But what happened next had his jaw drop open in surprise and confusion.

Trevor's face was suddenly filled with emotions, but it wasn't anger and hatred that twisted his features; it was despair and fear.

"Jennie's missing. She's my mate. Please help me find her."

Michael had no words, so he only nodded, and

before he regained the ability to speak, Trevor strode into the cottage, leaving him standing there in shock.

Michael's thoughts were a big, confused mass, and he was struggling to focus. *Jennie. Mate. Missing.* How? Why? What?!

He finally managed to move, and he almost ran into the cottage. "What do you mean she's missing? Did you hurt her?" Michael felt his anger building inside him, and he walked right up to the wolf. Taking on an alpha wolf was complete madness, but Jennie was worth ten of Michael, and she deserved someone standing up for her against the brute.

But again, Trevor surprised him.

"Yes, I hurt her. I should've fought for her, but instead I ran away like a coward." The anguish in the wolf's voice quenched Michael's anger instantly and made him take a step back in surprise.

"I'll help you look for her." To experience an alpha showing his fear and vulnerability like that was a shock to Michael. It was unheard of in his family and would probably be punished by death if it ever happened. But the thing that surprised Michael the most was how it increased his own respect for the wolf. Trevor was truly afraid for Jennie and didn't in any way try to hide how much that affected him.

"Thank you, Michael." Then Trevor looked around the room as he addressed all of them. "Let's split up and start our search."

Michael turned to look at his friends standing around the room and frowned when he caught James staring at him with an incredulous look on his face. His friend undoubtedly hadn't expected him to stand up for Jennie like that, and a few days ago, Michael probably wouldn't have. But if he was going to be able to stand up to his old man, it was time he stopped being a coward and took a stand for what he thought was right. Not that he was entirely clear on what that was yet, but hopefully, he would find out soon.

ooooo

They agreed to split up to search for Jennie. James, Carlos, and Michael would follow the shore going north along the route their group had been walking the other day. Jennie already knew that area, so it was likely she had chosen that direction.

Ann and Marna would look around the village and ask anyone they met if they had seen their friend. They had several pictures of Jennie on their phones that they could show to people in the village. Their husbands would have preferred their mates to stay at the cottage, but the women were adamant that they were going to help with the search, and James and Carlos knew better than to try to stop them.

Ann sent Trevor several photos of Jennie that he forwarded to Duncan. His friend was already out knocking on doors, but so far nobody had been able to tell him anything useful that could lead them to discover Jennie's whereabouts.

Trevor wanted to search on his own. Everyone knew not to shift during the daylight hours, but he wasn't going to adhere to that himself. If shifting could help him pick up Jennie's scent and pinpoint her location, nothing in this world would prevent him from changing into his wolf.

He followed the path from the cottage down

toward the sea loch. Just before reaching the shore, he stepped into the trees and removed his clothes. It only took him a second to change into his wolf form, and he immediately started searching for Jennie's most recent scent.

Judging by the faintness of her scent, she hadn't been in this area since the day before. While staying within the tree line so as not to be seen, Trevor followed the path they had taken to his house. Somewhere along that path on her way back from his house last night, she must have chosen a different direction. And he had to find that place and where she had headed. If he was able to follow her scent from there, he might be able to find her.

ooooo

Jennie was hungry and tired, but at least she had finally found out from which direction she had come last night. After some trial and error, she was certain she was on the correct path back toward the village.

She should be feeling relieved that she wasn't completely lost, but all Jennie felt was dread for what awaited her back in Fearolc. Or rather who didn't await her back there. Trevor had left and wasn't coming back, and knowing that left her with a hole inside her where her heart should have been. The world had lost all its color, and the only reason she was heading back at all was to make sure her friends weren't worried about her and to confront them about being wereanimals. They would be concerned when they discovered she wasn't with Trevor, and she wanted to know why they had kept her in the dark about what they were.

The sight of a huge wolf on the path in front of her cemented her feet to the ground, and terror seized her lungs and squeezed. Breathing became impossible, and she could only watch as the beast raced toward her to attack.

***

Trevor's relief at seeing Jennie was immense, and before he realized what he was doing, he started bounding toward her. But the sheer terror in her eyes had him grinding to a halt a few yards before reaching her.

This was it. He needed to go to her, but he couldn't do that as a wolf. And he couldn't leave her in order to change back into his human form. Jennie was his mate, and she had to get used to him being both a man and a wolf. This wasn't the way he had wanted to tell her about that, but there was no way around it at the moment.

It only took him a second to change into his human form, and he didn't waste time before running up to her and wrapping his arms around her in a tight embrace. "Jennie, I'm so sorry. I should never have left. I was a coward, afraid I'd get even more hurt if I stayed to confront you. Now I know you never agreed to be Michael's mate. Please forgive me."

Trevor was so happy to have her in his arms again that it took him a little while to realize she wasn't hugging him back. In fact, she was stiff as a board in his arms, and the fear rolling off her felt cloying and sickening.

He released her slowly and took a step back to give her a little space. Jennie's face was pale, her eyes wide with fear, and her heart rate was so fast even Nicko McBrain would have been impressed.

"I'm sorry, Jennie. I understand that it's a lot to take in. I shouldn't have rushed at you like that, but I'm just so relieved that you're okay. Please say something. Anything."

CHAPTER 23

Jennie had trouble focusing. Deep down she had known that Trevor was a wolf, but for some reason, the implications of that had eluded her. Ever since she had seen the werewolves in the forest earlier, she had known her friends were some kind of wereanimal. Her brain had also touched on the fact that Trevor must be a wolf, but without really understanding what that entailed.

Trevor's dog was, of course, not a dog. It was Trevor, and not a dog at all but a wolf. The fact that she had slept with a wolf was just…something she didn't know how to deal with at the moment, so she was going to push that to the back of her brain. It would probably come back to haunt her later.

"Jennie. Jennie!" Trevor's commanding voice reached her, and she realized he had probably spoken to her for a while, trying to get her attention. At least he hadn't changed back into a wolf yet.

She took a careful step back to put a little more

space between them, and silently tried to talk her heart into calming down. Wild animals could sense fear, and it would bring out their urge to hunt. Not a good thing at the moment.

"Jennie, please. Say something. I didn't mean to scare you." Trevor's voice was pleading, and he sounded hurt, but Jennie hadn't regained the ability to speak yet, and even if she had, what was there to say? What could she possibly say to a lover who changed into a wolf, a creature even more terrifying than a dog?

She just shook her head at him slowly and took another step back away from him.

The stark pain in Trevor's eyes was a bit distressing, but it didn't change the fact of what he was. Her friends might also be were-something-or-other, but at least they weren't wolves. If she could just get back to them, they might be able to help her make sense of all of this.

***

Trevor watched Jennie slowly back away from him in fear, like she was trying to prevent awakening his instinct to hunt. He didn't know what to do other than to let her go. Moving toward her would only increase her fear of him even more, and he had already tried talking to her. Trevor wanted to fight to secure her as his mate, but he had no idea how. Brute strength wasn't the appropriate method in this case. If anything, it would only make things worse. His only option was to back away and give her some space. Maybe then she would calm down enough to think rationally. Not that rational had anything to do with this situation.

At least he had to make sure she got back to the village all right. "Jennie. The village is in the direction I came from." Trevor slowly moved off the path while talking to her calmly, trying to encourage her to start moving toward Fearolc instead of backing away in the opposite direction. He kept moving until he was a good distance off to the side of the track. "Please Jennie, go to your friends in the village. They're worried about you."

Jennie stopped, and he knew she had heard him and acknowledged the truth of what he was saying.

"They're waiting for you, Jennie. Marna almost had a full-on panic attack when she realized that you had been gone all night, and Ann… Let's just say that it's a good thing you're not hurt, because she'd try to kill whoever hurt you."

Jennie took one step forward and then another while eyeing him like he was likely to pounce on her at any moment. Trevor kept completely still and tried to relax his body in order to seem as nonthreatening as possible.

When she finally walked past him and continued down the path and into the trees, Trevor couldn't hold it together any longer. He fell to his knees and changed into his wolf before running in the opposite direction of Jennie. He needed to get away. Far away. He just couldn't face the reality of what had just happened.

ထထထ

It took Jennie almost two hours to get back to the cottage, and when she stepped into the kitchen, Ann and Marna practically attacked her. They were both laughing and crying, and Jennie was a little surprised at just how worried they had been about her.

"It's so good to see you're okay. Where have you been? We thought something might've happened to you." Ann looked at her with a mixture of joy and concern in her eyes.

"Everyone's out looking for you. We just came back from asking around the village if anyone had seen you." Marna had tears staining her cheeks, but she was smiling.

Jennie sighed. "I'm sorry. I shouldn't have run off like that. Everything kind of blacked out for me for a while, and when I finally emerged from the fog in my brain, I was lost, and it was getting dark. I didn't want to try to find my way back in the dark, so I found a place to sleep for a while until it got light. I forgot my cell phone in my room, but out there I probably wouldn't have gotten reception anyway. I'm sorry you've been so worried. It wasn't my intention to scare you."

Ann shook her head and chuckled. "We know, but of course we started worrying when Trevor came by this morning, looking for you, and woke us all up. He's really worried that something happened to you. You should call him and let him know you're okay."

Jennie swallowed and looked away. For a minute she had forgotten what her friends were, but the mention of Trevor brought it all back.

"I've already seen him." She looked at Ann. "I met him on my way back."

"Oh." Ann frowned. "You don't seem happy about that. I thought you liked him. Are you still angry with him for leaving? He explained when he came here this morning. He's really sorry, you know. You should give him another chance."

Jennie sighed and shook her head. Her hunger and exhaustion came back with a vengeance, but there was no way she could stomach food at the moment. She should just go to bed and sleep, but she needed to talk to Ann and Marna. And since their husbands were gone, it was the best time.

Instead of responding to Ann about Trevor, she launched into her own questioning. "Why didn't you tell me you're some kind of wereanimal?" Jennie looked at both her friends to judge their reactions. "Yes, I know werewolves exist now. I've seen them with my own eyes. And I know you're were-something-or-other as well. I just don't know what kind."

Both Ann and Marna were staring back at her with wide eyes. Ann snapped out of it first, but the denial Jennie was expecting didn't come.

"Thank God, you've figured it out. I've wanted to tell you for so long, but I haven't been allowed. Only people mated to a shifter or close family can be let in on the secret, and you being neither…" Ann let the sentence hang.

"So, what are you?" Jennie stared at her friends. The people she was closest to in this world, and who until last night she had thought she knew so well.

Ann chuckled. "We are human." She indicated herself and Marna. "But our husbands, or mates as it's called in the shifter world, are wereservals."

Jennie frowned. "But isn't it contagious or something? Wouldn't you become wereservals as well, when you…you know, mate?"

Ann shook her head, smiling. "No, it doesn't work like that. You have to be born a shifter, it's not something you can become. That's only in the movies."

"But they can mate with humans and have children, or whatever shifter babies are called?"

Both Ann and Marna nodded.

"Yes." Marna was smiling. "But mating doesn't just mean sex, it's the bond between two people. Marriage has nothing on mating, trust me. The bond between mates is much deeper, and it can't be broken by signing a paper. It's for life. And it gives sex a whole other dimension. You have no idea." The wicked smile on Marna's face was unusual for her. She was normally the more modest of Jennie's friends.

"So." Jennie was trying to sum up what she had learned. "James and Carlos are both wereservals, and you are their mates. What about Michael? I guess he's one as well?"

Ann nodded. "Yes, and if he wasn't such a dick, perhaps you guys would've hit it off. If you had agreed to become his mate, we'd finally been able to reveal the shifter secret to you. It would've been a big relief, and of course, we really wanted you to find the kind of happiness that we've found with our mates. Particularly after what that asshole Olivier did to you."

"But that's all sorted now." Marna smiled happily at her. There were even fresh tears in her eyes. "Now that you've found your own true mate."

Jennie's jaw fell open in disbelief. They still expected her to mate Michael? After all that had happened?

Before she found the words to respond, however, Ann continued where Marna had stopped.

"Trevor told us, and we're so happy for you. You

have to forgive him for running away. He thought you had agreed to become Michael's mate, and it took Trevor a little while to realize that you're actually his mate. But he's—"

"Stop!" Jennie couldn't listen to this. It was just too crazy. "I'm not anyone's mate, and particularly not someone who can turn into a wolf. I should've known he was too good to be true. Just knowing that I've been in bed with him…"

She turned around to get away, and crashed right into a hard, wide chest. Dread filled her and she took a step back. Raising her head, she stared directly into Duncan's concerned eyes. Then, he swung his gaze around the room before returning it to her.

"Where's Trevor?"

Jennie could only shake her head at him.

"He doesn't know you're back and okay?" Duncan narrowed his eyes at her. "I'd better call and tell him then."

"Don't bother." Jennie averted her eyes and sighed. She didn't want to explain. All she wanted was to hide in her room and go to sleep for a really long time.

"Trevor needs to know you're okay. He's been out of his mind with worry."

Jennie looked up at him then. She had to face this head on. "He knows. I met him on my way back. He knows I'm fine."

"Then, where is he?" Duncan's face seemed intentionally devoid of any emotion, but it was like concern and anger were radiating off him.

"I don't know. Maybe back at his house? I didn't exactly ask what his plans were for the day." Jennie was getting annoyed. Everyone suddenly expected her to be with Trevor, like it was a done deal or something. But she wasn't some creature's plaything to do with as it pleased. "Now if you'll excuse me." She tried to move around him to get to the door, but he intentionally moved into her path, effectively stopping her.

"What did you say to him? It must've been something horrible to prevent him from following you here." Duncan's eyes were cold when they looked at her, but there was an underlying fury there that scared Jennie more than she wanted to admit. She had no doubt this man or wolf could be lethal if pushed too far. It had her backing up a couple of steps away from him.

"A wolf who's found his true mate doesn't leave her side until they're mated, and even then it usually takes a while for him to be able to let her out of his sight for more than a few minutes." Duncan stepped toward her, closing the gap between them. "I want to know what you said to him."

His voice had taken on a bit of a growl, and Jennie felt the hair at the back of her neck stand up as her mind started shutting down in fear. Her vision narrowed down to focus on Duncan's teeth. His large canines seemed to grow even longer as she watched.

It suddenly felt like time was standing still, and she was at the other end of the room, observing this scene from someone else's perspective. The large scary wolfman and the terrified woman. The wolfman was going to attack the woman at any moment, tear into her with his teeth as blood sprayed across the wall. It would all be over in seconds. The woman didn't stand a chance. She would be dead and gone before ever being able to put up a fight.

Jennie frowned as there was an unexpected turn of events. Everything happened so fast it was a bit of a blur. Duncan was yanked back and disappeared out the door, landing on his back with something large standing over him, gripping his throat. She had seen that large wolf before and should have been terrified, but the fierce growl it was making was doing strange things to her body. It was like a balm to her frayed nerves, soothing and alleviating her fear. At the same time, her body lit up with a fire inside her so intense she was instantly wet and aching to have Trevor inside her. Without realizing it, Jennie had moved outside to soak up even more of that growl and the power flowing over her like silk.

***

Duncan was lying completely still, and Trevor wasn't going to hurt him in any way. But he was pissed at Duncan for scaring his mate. Her fear had been so intense he'd had no choice but to intervene, even though he had planned to stay away from her for a while to let her rest and get over the initial shock of seeing him as a wolf.

After the intense agony at having Jennie shrink away from him in fear, all he had wanted to do was run. But it didn't take him long to understand he was about to make the same mistake twice. The only way to make her his was to help her overcome her fear of him. She had liked him as a man before she knew he was a wolf, so there had to be a way to help her remember that. It might take a long time, but he was willing to put in the time and effort necessary to gain his true mate.

An amazing scent wafted past Trevor's nose and had him drooling all over Duncan's throat. His dick started throbbing, and he let go of Duncan to look around for the source of the most amazing scent he had ever smelled in his entire life. The sight of his mate standing not two yards away, staring at him with her eyes shining with arousal, almost had him rolling over on his back and exposing his throat to her. Whether or not Jennie liked him, she had control over him. Always and forever.

Instead of lying down on his back, Trevor changed into his human form and faced her. He wanted to step up to her and take her in his arms, but since that might scare her, he stood completely still, leaving the decision of what to do next up to her.

Jennie's gaze moved slowly over his naked body, from his head to his feet, before zooming in on his groin. He almost squirmed he was so hot for her—his cock throbbing so hard it felt like it had its very own heart. His balls were pulled up tight, and all he could think about was how good it would feel to thrust into her tight wet channel.

Anger suddenly flashed in Jennie's eyes, and she turned and placed herself between him and the door to the cottage, where Ann and Marna were standing, staring at them. "Cover yourself for fuck's sake. The whole world doesn't need to see you like that."

Trevor put both his hands in front of his crotch to try to cover his very erect member. It was all he could do since he didn't have any clothes nearby. A small smile stole across his face at Jennie's possessive behavior, and he felt his heart soar at the small sign that she might want him after all.

"Well, some clothes may be in order." Without Trevor noticing, Duncan had gotten to his feet and was standing a few yards to his right.

CHAPTER 24

The amusement in Duncan's voice had Jennie glaring at him over her shoulder. "This is funny to you? Go find him some clothes!"

Duncan's eyes widened, and he took a step back like someone had pushed him. Then he nodded. "Yes, ma'am."

"If you follow the path down to the shore, my clothes are just within the trees on the right."

Trevor's voice from behind her caressed along her spine, and Jennie shivered. It was scaring her how much he affected her, but for some reason, she wasn't nearly as afraid of him as before. Which was a bit frightening all by itself.

Jennie narrowed her eyes at her friends still standing in the doorway to the cottage. "Go back inside!" She had no idea where this hostility was coming from, but just the thought of Ann and Marna, or anyone else for that matter, seeing Trevor naked had her anger spiking.

Her friends quickly disappeared into the cottage, and Jennie's shoulders sagged in relief. She breathed a little easier.

"Thank you."

She sucked in a breath at the sound of Trevor's voice. How could a voice be so tangible, like something physically touching her body?

Jennie slowly turned around and met Trevor's warm brown eyes. "What for?"

"For protecting my dignity." Amusement stole over his face, even though it seemed like he was trying to hide it.

Her anger spiked again, and she took a step toward him, putting them almost chest to chest. "What? You wanted them to look at you, show them all you've got?"

The amusement was gone from Trevor's face in an instant, and his hands came up like he was at gunpoint. "I… No! I—"

"These." Jennie gripped his stiff cock and cupped his balls. "Are mine. And mine only."

Trevor nodded with a look of pure rapture on his face, and Jennie suddenly realized what she was doing.

***

Things changed so fast it took Trevor a few seconds to understand what was happening. One second Jennie was gripping his cock with the most glorious possessive look on her face, and the next she was releasing him like he was a lump of red-hot coal and stepping back with a look of horror on her face. Before he even had a chance to process what was going on, she was running away from him.

"Jennie," he yelled just as she rounded the corner

of the cottage, and by the time he reached the corner, he heard her trying to close the damaged door to her room.

Trevor slowed down and took a deep breath. Whatever had just happened was progress, even if she had just run from him again. She was possessive of him and aroused by him protecting her. This was true mate behavior and meant that she was feeling the effects of the bond between them just like he was. The bond wasn't fully developed yet, but it was stronger than he had thought possible without them actually mating.

He walked to her door but made no move to open it. It was a little ajar due to the damage he had inflicted earlier.

"Jennie, I'm sorry. You must be very confused and scared at the moment, and I understand that. What you're experiencing is mating behavior. It's nothing to be afraid of."

Trevor waited a little to let Jennie respond, but there wasn't a sound from inside her room.

"Whenever you're ready to talk, come and see me. I won't push you into anything you don't want, Jennie. You're worth more to me than anything else in the world, and I'd never intentionally hurt you. But please understand that what we can have together is unique. Not many shifters find their true mates, and those who do are envied by all for the special bond they share."

He wanted to open the door to see her and judge her reaction to what he was saying, but he didn't. Trevor had promised not to push her, and he was going to honor that promise even if it killed him.

"I'll be at home if you need to talk."

He had to force his body to move away from her door. Everything inside him was driving him to stay near her and mate with her, but he had to leave her alone to come to terms with everything that was happening to her.

Duncan stood a few yards away with an unreadable expression on his face. He handed Trevor his clothes without a word and Trevor dressed quickly.

"Come." He looked at Duncan before starting to walk away from the cottage.

Duncan fell into step with him, and they walked for a couple of minutes in silence.

"You're just going to leave her there to fend for herself?"

Trevor turned his head and met Duncan's eyes, which were looking back at him with concern and a little sadness.

Trevor shrugged. "I can't force her to mate with me, Duncan. It has to happen because she wants it to happen as well. Jennie's everything to me, and I want nothing more than to mate her right this second. But because she means that much to me, I need to let her come to me. There's no doubt she's already feeling the mating bond, and hopefully that will be enough to help her overcome her fear of my wolf and the fear of loving someone again."

Duncan frowned. "Why would Jennie be afraid of loving you? She seems like a person who cares a lot about other people."

"She has gone through a divorce, and I've got a strong feeling that it wasn't her actions that led to the destruction of her marriage. Jennie was hurt and betrayed by someone she trusted and cared about. It has left deeper scars than I think she realizes. And now she feels betrayed not only by me, but by her friends, for keeping the world of shifters a secret from her. Jennie needs time to deal with that. She's a rational and intelligent woman, so deep down she knows that there's a good reason why she couldn't be told. But that doesn't prevent it from feeling like a betrayal by the people she trusts the most."

Duncan shook his head in disbelief. "I don't think I'd be able to be so calm in your situation. If it was my mate acting like this, I'd probably sit outside her door, howling until she got so fed up with the sound that she let me in. There's no way I'd be able to stay away from her."

Trevor couldn't help the corner of his mouth pulling up in a small smile. "Sounds like you're ready to find your mate."

"No! Fuck no! And this is exactly why. I don't want a woman to have that kind of power over me. Free will is a great thing, and I intend to keep it that way. I love fucking women, but I don't linger after we're done, and I always make sure they know and accept that before I touch them."

Trevor studied his friend's face before turning his head back to see where he was going. Duncan had never had a relationship with a woman beyond sex that Trevor knew of, and he had never thought it odd in any way before. It wasn't uncommon behavior for young shifter males, or human males for that matter. But he was starting to wonder if there was a reason for Duncan's behavior, something in his past that Trevor didn't know about. Duncan loved all the pups living in this area and happily spent time with them, teaching them everything they needed to know to become strong and honorable wolves, from mending fences to fighting techniques. So it didn't seem to be a fear of raising a family that was preventing Duncan from wanting more from a woman than sex. On the contrary, Trevor had seen some evidence that Duncan longed for pups of his own.

Pups. Trevor wondered how Jennie would feel about having pups. He would love to see her belly grow with his young, and he would love to put them there. The thought made him more aware of his still very hard cock, and the need to mate with Jennie that still simmered in his whole body. His testicles felt like two steal balls between his legs, making walking uncomfortable. But he knew that even if he spent the rest of the day and all night jerking off, it wouldn't alleviate his condition. Only mating Jennie or having his dick fall off would help. Perhaps this was the real reason wolves that were denied their true mates often ended up taking their own lives. He imagined the pain would be unbearable after a while. Hopefully, Jennie would come to him before that happened.

ooooo

Jennie had no idea how long she had been sitting in her room, staring at the wall, when she heard her stomach growling. It was loud, telling her in no uncertain terms that she was hungry.

She sighed. Her thoughts were going in all directions, and she didn't know how to make sense of everything that had happened in the last twenty-four hours. She had discovered a whole other world of beings, or rather the world she thought she had known consisted of so much more than she had ever imagined. What was she going to write about when all the supernatural beings she liked writing about had turned out to be real? Well, she didn't know that yet. Some of them might actually be just fiction. At least she hoped so, because she didn't want to meet an actual living vampire. Or dead or undead or whatever they really were.

Jennie stood up from where she had been sitting on her bed and immediately became aware of how wet and achy she still was. An image in her mind of Trevor standing naked, looking at her with desire dancing in his eyes, had her shuddering. The sight of his huge, swollen cock throbbing between his legs had burned itself into her retinas, and the thought of how it would feel to have it fill her made her gasp and squirm. That was when she realized both her hands were down her panties, working herself toward release.

She was a bit shocked by her own actions. Not that she was masturbating, but that she was doing it with the door ajar and the curtains open. Jennie couldn't stop, though. She needed the release more than her next breath. A few seconds later and she almost screamed as a powerful orgasm rolled through her. She had to lock her knees to keep standing.

Jennie breathed a sigh of relief when the strong climax subsided, and she pulled her hands out of her panties. She hadn't taken more than a few steps, though, when her clit started throbbing like she was over halfway there to another orgasm.

She closed her eyes in disbelief. What was it that Trevor had said? That what she was experiencing was mating behavior. Jennie guessed that included the extreme horniness and not just the jealousy and possessiveness from before.

But she didn't want to mate him, did she? She thought of the massive wolf standing over Duncan gripping his throat with its powerful jaws, but the fear she had felt when she first laid eyes on Trevor in his wolf form didn't surface. Instead, the beauty of that beast struck her for the first time, and how good it had felt to have him protect her.

Jennie shook her head to try to get out of the trance she was in. She must be possessed or something. This just wasn't how she would normally feel or act. And she needed to think and not feel at the moment, to figure out what she was going to do about all this.

But all she really wanted to do was go to Trevor. Throw herself in his arms and stay there. Jennie could think of nothing she wanted more.

Mentally giving herself a slap, she tried to focus on what she needed to do. The rest of her life was at stake, and she wasn't going to rush into anything without taking some time to think. Even though her body had already decided it wanted Trevor, her mind was stronger.

Jennie needed a shower, and she needed food. Those two things became her mantra as she found new clothes and her toiletries and headed for the shower.

Ann and Marna were still in the kitchen when she entered, but she firmly held up her hand to indicate she wasn't going to talk to them. Shower first, then food. She could talk to them while she ate.

Standing under the hot spray of water felt good,

and it was the first time since she got back that her heart rate slowed to somewhere near her normal pulse. She washed her hair and body, but cleaning between her legs brought her heart rate right back up. It only took a few times of her fingers touching her clit before an orgasm ripped through her, and she had yet another one while rinsing off. So much for the shower calming her down.

After carefully toweling off, she got dressed and went into the kitchen. Ann and Marna sat at the kitchen table, and they both looked up when she walked in.

Jennie sighed. "I'm sorry about earlier. I didn't mean to command you around. I just..." She didn't know how to explain it without acknowledging that she was feeling possessive of Trevor, like her friends were potential rivals.

Ann laughed. "Oh, we understand perfectly. We're both like that with our men."

Marna smiled happily and nodded. "I think I'd happily kill her if a woman saw Carlos naked, and then I'd plead insanity."

Jennie chuckled. That was how she felt about Trevor. It was a good thing it was her best friends who had seen Trevor in that state, and not some other women. She would have likely killed them. Ann and Marna were happily married and mated, and she knew they had no interest in Trevor whatsoever. It still nagged her that they had seen him naked, but she could live with that.

She went to the fridge and pulled out ingredients for a sandwich. While she was preparing her food, she heard noises outside, and then the kitchen was suddenly invaded by the guys coming back from looking for her.

James, Carlos, and Michael all looked relieved to see her, but questions about Trevor and why she wasn't with her mate had her fleeing to her room.

She'd had about all she could take of questions and advice and expectations for one day. She wanted to think and make up her own mind about all this, and not be bullied into what was the right thing to do according to everyone else.

After eating her sandwich and drinking a glass of juice, Jennie lay down on her bed. Her body was still trying to convince her to go to Trevor, but she was more in charge after having eaten and restored some of her energy.

What was the worst thing that could happen if she agreed to mate Trevor? Would he get tired of her after a while and find someone else, or was it true like Marna had said that mating was forever? She didn't really know what to believe, but she found the idea of being mated to Trevor for the rest of her life appealing. He was an amazing man, not to mention fantastic in bed.

But he wasn't just a man. He was a shifter, a werewolf, and she didn't know much about real werewolves. Well, she might know a little about them. James and Carlos were shifters, as well, and there were probably some similarities between wereservals and werewolves. Ann and Marna had both blossomed after meeting their mates, and even after three years together, they were still acting like newlyweds.

Would it be like that for her and Trevor? Her body was saying yes, but she still wasn't convinced. And how would she be able to live with someone who could turn into a wolf at any time? She was able to see the beauty of the animal, but would she ever be able to be close to it? And was it really an "it" at all when it was Trevor? She had no idea what went on in a werewolf's brain. Did it think human thoughts, or was it mostly driven by instincts?

Somewhere in the middle of all her thoughts and questions, Jennie fell asleep.

CHAPTER 25

It was early evening and Trevor had tried almost everything to forget her or ease the need running rampant in his body. Walking was painful, so he had tried watching TV, but nothing could hold his interest for long, and his thoughts quickly returned to Jennie. He had taken a shower and jerked off a couple of times, but instead of bringing him some relief, it had actually made it worse.

He was just about ready to give in to his urge to go down to the Miller's cottage and plead with Jennie to mate him, when there was a knock on the backdoor. Careful not to get his hopes up, he got up from the recliner and walked a little straddle-legged to the backdoor. He wasn't dressed and only wore a towel wrapped around his hips, but whoever it was would just have to ignore that.

The sight of Jennie standing there with her long blond hair mussed from sleep almost had his knees buckle. He had never seen anything more beautiful in his life.

"Jennie." His voice came out rough, like he hadn't spoken for a long time.

"I need some answers." She was looking at him almost apologetically, and there was fear in her eyes.

He gave her a small smile, telling himself this was a good sign. If she had totally dismissed the idea of mating him, she wouldn't have come to him at all. "Well, you'd better come in then."

"I'm not sure that's a good idea." She took a step back away from him.

Trevor inwardly sighed. Jennie was still skittish. He had hoped that her coming to him meant she had gotten over some of her fear of him, but seeing her reaction he wasn't so sure. It might be just her body driving her to be near him, and he needed more than the cooperation of her body to mate her. She had to want him with her heart and mind.

"Please don't be scared of me, Jennie. We can sit in the kitchen. I'll answer your questions, and then you can leave if that's what you want."

She looked doubtful for a few seconds, but then she seemed to steel herself and gave him a little nod.

He let the door stay open and turned around to lead the way into the kitchen. It would probably make her feel more comfortable following him than having him behind her.

Trevor sat down at the kitchen table and waited for Jennie to settle opposite him. She was clearly in doubt of whether she should be there or not, and he didn't want to push her decision toward not being there, so he kept silent and waited for her to start.

***

Jennie felt as though her body was crawling with ants but in a good way. Just the sight of Trevor had eased some of the crazy chaos in her body, like this was where she was meant to be. With him. But the need within her hadn't diminished, and the sight of him standing in the doorway with only a towel wrapped around his hips had almost floored her. Every part of his body from his face to his toes was perfection, and she wanted to rip that towel from his body and launch herself into his arms. They could be fucking like bunnies within seconds.

The feel of wetness soaking through her panties had the images fading, and she somehow managed to follow him into the kitchen without touching him.

Sitting down opposite him at the kitchen table, she tried to gather her thoughts. There was a reason why she was there, and that was to get answers. Trevor was obviously waiting for her to start, so she asked him the first question that came to mind.

"Why am I so fucking horny all the time? And it doesn't stop no matter what I..." Jennie trailed off as she realized what she was saying. This wasn't one of the questions she had intended to ask.

Trevor's eyes seemed to glow with desire, and the corners of his mouth pulled up into a smile so devastatingly wicked that her pussy clamped down, and she almost came from just looking at him.

"What have you done to try to make it stop?" Trevor's voice was filled with gravel as he stared at her with desire pouring off him.

"I... Um. Never mind that." Jennie couldn't look away from him. "I have other questions."

"Shoot."

Jennie licked her dry lips. Trevor still had that devilish smile on his face, and it was making it hard for her to think.

"Would you still want me in five years or ten? Or does this need we feel for each other wear off after a little while?"

Trevor's wicked smile changed to one that could easily be mistaken for love, and it was no less devastating than the smile he had given her a few seconds ago.

"Mating is forever, Jennie. It doesn't matter how long we live. We will always want each other. There will never be another woman for me. Just the thought is repulsive. There's only you, and I'll always love you."

"It's a bit early to talk about love, isn't it? We just met." It seemed too good to be true that Trevor loved her, so it probably was. Love might develop over time. She could accept and even believe that, but not so soon.

Trevor shook his head, still smiling. "Not for me, it isn't. I think I fell in love with you the first time I met you. When you gave me that amazing smile on the plane, I was sold. It just took me a few days to comprehend that it was more than lust I was feeling for you."

Jennie didn't know what to say. Trevor loved her, and she should be scared that this was all happening too fast, but her heart was soaring. She had already recognized that the feelings she had for Trevor were much stronger than anything she had ever felt for Olivier. But love? Was she already in love with this man? And wolf? Which reminded her of her next question.

"What happens when you're a wolf? Are you still able to think? Like a human, I mean?" Jennie was a bit apprehensive about asking this, but she had to know.

Trevor chuckled and she relaxed a little. At least he wasn't annoyed with her for asking.

"I'm still me even when I'm a wolf. We're the same, and I'm capable of rational thought no matter which form I take. The difference lies in what each body is capable of. My wolf has better senses, and I'm faster and more agile in my wolf form. My human body has hands, and of course, I can talk in my human form. And because I'm a shifter, I'm stronger, faster, and have better senses than a human male."

Well, at least he wasn't just an animal when he looked like a wolf. Jennie was relieved to hear that.

"Do you want something to drink?" Trevor got up and moved over to the fridge.

Jennie frowned when she saw Trevor wincing when he stood, and she couldn't help but noticing the way he walked. His legs were a little wider apart than usual, and it seemed uncomfortable for him to move around. She had noticed the clear outline of his big erect cock when he opened the door, and she had understood that he was suffering from the same effects that she was. But she hadn't realized the level of pain he was in.

"Jennie?" Trevor was looking at her over his shoulder, and she remembered he had asked her if she wanted something to drink.

"Yes, a glass of juice would be nice."

She studied him while he moved around by the counter before coming back to the table, carrying two glasses of juice. All this pain and need and love, and he still hadn't tried to push her into mating him. He was waiting for her to make up her own mind, leaving his own fate and happiness in her hands. The realization brought tears to her eyes.

"Jennie? What's wrong?" The concern in Trevor's voice brought her gaze to his, and in that instant, she knew exactly what she wanted.

She stood at the same time Trevor put the glasses on the table.

"Yes."

Trevor frowned, looking confused. "Yes, something's wrong?"

Jennie shook her head at him and tried again. "Yes, I'll be your mate."

The emotions shooting across Trevor's face was amazing to watch. From confusion, to surprise, to careful hope and budding joy. "Are you sure?"

Instead of answering, she rounded the table and grabbed his hand, pulling him after her out of the kitchen and down the hall toward the stairs. Trevor followed without a word as they mounted the stairs and continued to his big bedroom.

Jennie didn't stop until they were standing next to Trevor's bed. Then, she turned to him and in one swift move, she ripped the towel from his body.

"Jennie." Trevor's voice was all gravel, and his big muscular body was trembling.

Jennie ripped her own clothes off before pushing Trevor backward until he sat down on the bed. She put one knee on the bed on each side of his lap and was about to lower herself down onto him when he grabbed her thighs and stopped her.

A little confused, she looked into his eyes.

"Jennie, I have to be sure. Are you certain you want

to mate me?" The hope and love in his eyes were so stark, but the fact that he had actually stopped her to make sure she really wanted this was what convinced her of his love for her.

"Yes, Trevor. I want this. I want you. I love you." And she did. There was no doubt in her mind or heart anymore. There might never have been any doubt in her heart, she just hadn't recognized it.

He let go of her thighs and moved his hands up to her waist as she lowered herself onto his thick cock. The feeling of him stretching and filling her was even more amazing than she remembered.

***

Jennie's tight channel gripped him as he sank into her wet heat. She didn't stop until she had taken all of him, and Trevor groaned with pleasure. This was going to be over in seconds. His balls were pulled up so tight he could almost feel them lodged in his throat.

He reached down to fondle her clit as she started moving up and down him, and she whimpered and gripped his shoulders tightly with her hands.

Trevor let her move up and down him a few times before he lifted them both up, turned around, and laid Jennie down on her back on the bed. Still inside her, he started moving, before a moment of clarity allowed him to realize she didn't know what the act of mating entailed.

"Jennie." He could hardly talk anymore.

"Um." Jennie was obviously as far gone as he was.

He tried to stop moving to be able to tell her what she needed to know, but all he managed to do was slow down a little.

"I need to tell you."

"What?" The word was barely distinguishable from a breath.

"To mate you I'll have to bite you, but it'll feel good."

Jennie froze up in his arms, and Trevor finally managed to stop moving.

Her eyes were wide when she looked at him. "You'll change into a wolf?"

"No! My teeth will lengthen a bit. That's all. My bite will increase your pleasure. And I've heard that my dick might get a little thicker."

Jennie looked relived. Then she chuckled. "I hope not too much thicker. You might get stuck."

Trevor breathed out a sigh of relief. Then, he started moving again. "Getting stuck inside you sounds like heaven."

There was no more stopping. The drive to mate was so strong his vision blurred, and all he felt was the need and the mounting pleasure, in both of them. He could feel that Jennie was close to climaxing, and he adjusted the angle of his strokes until he felt her body stiffen in the grip of impending ecstasy. Then he lowered his mouth to her shoulder. And as she screamed her pleasure, he bit down hard across her clavicle and shoulder.

His own climax roared through him. Jennie's already tight channel seemed to tighten even more around him, causing him to spill so hard he almost blacked out from the sheer pleasure. Jennie screamed again, her body convulsing in another powerful orgasm, brought on by his bite that bound them together forever. It was the happiest moment of his life.

***

Jennie's body was still buzzing with the aftereffects of the most powerful orgasms she had ever had in her life. She wasn't quite ready to move yet, but she opened her eyes to stare directly into two warm brown ones. And the love shining in those eyes felt like it poured into her body it was so strong.

"How do you feel?" Trevor's rough voice made her shiver as it caressed her skin. He was still on top of her, but he was using his elbows to support his body to prevent his weight from crushing her.

She sighed happily. "Amazing. And a little odd."

Trevor had a small smile on his lips. "What do you mean odd?"

"It's like some of your feelings kind of overflow into me. I don't know how to explain it. I've never felt anything like it before. It might just be a result of you being such a fantastic lover."

Trevor chuckled. "We're true mates. It's common to feel your mate's feelings, at least when they're strong. That's something that usually develops over time, though. I've never heard of it happening immediately after mating."

"Can you feel what I'm feeling as well?" Jennie stared into Trevor's beautiful eyes, and her heart almost erupted with the love she felt for this man. Wolf. Shifter. It didn't bother her anymore what he was. He was gorgeous and he was hers.

He nodded. "Yes, and I'm the luckiest man alive. Now, what do you want to do the rest of the night?"

Jennie gasped when Trevor rolled his pelvis toward her, and his swollen cock filled her up all the way to her core. She was more than ready for him, but this time she wanted to be in the driver's seat.

"Roll." She pushed on his chest, and he happily obliged.

Straddling him, she slowly started moving up and down while rotating her pelvis and squeezing him with her vaginal muscles. The groans and growls he was making made her body shiver with her need for release, and she put one hand on his chest to steady herself while using her other hand to fondle her clit.

Trevor's eyes homed in on her hand playing with herself, and the continuous growl he was making brought her closer to the edge by the second.

Jennie could feel Trevor's impending climax through their bond. He was getting close.

"You're not allowed to come yet." She whispered the words, but it almost felt like a shout in the room.

Trevor's eyes flew up to hers, and they were wide with surprise. "I won't last much longer. Watching you pleasure yourself is driving me crazy."

Jennie gave him a wicked smile, and started whimpering and groaning while riding him harder and continuing to let her fingers play with her clit.

"Jennie." Trevor's voice was pained, and he was panting. "Please."

His hands came up to fondle her breasts, and he suddenly pinched her nipples at the same time as he drove his cock hard into her from below. The climax she had been holding off to increase their pleasure crashed through her body, and she heard Trevor roar as his cock jerked inside her. She felt his climax backing up her own, increasing and extending the pleasure, and wave after wave of shear ecstasy kept rolling through her body.

Jennie was exhausted by the time they came back to reality. She was lying on Trevor's chest, panting like she had just run a marathon in two hours flat, uphill. "Holy fuck. That was out of this world. Was that a mate thing?"

Trevor answered while breathing hard. "Yes, I agree. And yes, I think that was a mate thing."

"Well, in that case I think we'll be doing that again. Just not right now."

Jennie could hear Trevor's chest rumble with laughter as she fell into sleep.

EPILOGUE

It was Saturday morning, and Jennie and Trevor had gone down to the Miller's cottage to see her friends off to Edinburgh. The last day had passed by in a blur for Jennie. She and Trevor had been so wrapped up in each other they had hardly had time to get out of bed to eat. In between the lovemaking, there had been a lot of talking and touching. And even after all that, Jennie had trouble staying more than two feet away from Trevor. Her heart rate sped up whenever he was out of touching distance. Apparently, it was a mate thing, and Trevor was feeling it as well, so they walked around like they were glued together most of the time.

Trevor had assured her that it would fade a bit over time. They would be able to spend a little time apart. But the mating bond would always pull them together, and any length of time apart would be difficult. Usually that wasn't a problem, since mates rarely wanted to stay apart. They did everything together.

"I'm going to miss you." Ann was looking at her

with tears in her eyes. "But at least I know that you're happy and well taken care of."

"I am, and he does." Heat ran through her as she turned to look at Trevor. He was talking to James not two yards away, but Jennie still wanted to go to him and press her body tightly against his side.

"Ah, newly mated. I remember what that was like." Ann chuckled.

Jennie looked back at her friend and couldn't help the grin that spread across her face. "I'm so happy for you, too, Ann. Now I know what you have with James, and that you're truly happy. Not that there has ever been any indication that you were not, but I've been a bit worried with how fast you guys got married. Now I understand why. When you find your true mate, that's it."

Jennie turned to look at Marna as she came into the room with her small backpack and purse. Carlos was following close behind with the last of their luggage. "And Marna as well. To know both of you are happily mated." Tears blurred Jennie's vision as she looked back at Ann. "I couldn't ask for anything better for you two."

They gave each other a fierce hug, and while they were still holding each other, Marna came over and hugged the both of them.

"Please come visit soon, okay?" Marna's voice was choked with her crying.

"We will. After our honeymoon."

They let go of each other.

"Where are you going?" Marna was looking at her with her eyes shining with tears, but there was a happy smile on her face.

"We're staying here. I want to get to know this place. Perhaps we'll travel a bit around Scotland, if we can get out of bed long enough."

Both her friends laughed.

"Yeah, there's that. But just a little warning." Marna stared at her, narrowing her eyes. "The sex gets even better with time, when you learn to use the mating bond for all it's worth." Marna's eyes twinkled with amusement. "So, it doesn't get any easier getting out of bed."

"I second that." Carlos put his arms around his wife and pulled her firmly to him with her back against his front. "And if you keep talking like that, I might have to take you back to bed."

Jennie burst out laughing. It was great seeing her friends like this. They had been really close ever since high school, but lately it had felt like they were starting to drift apart. It was easy to understand why, since there was a part of their lives they'd had to keep a secret from her. But that wasn't an issue anymore, and their friendship had returned and was even stronger than before. They could truly have each other's backs again.

ooooo

They were walking hand in hand back to Trevor's house, which was actually their house. It wasn't legally sorted out yet, but Trevor had been very clear on the fact that mates shared everything. There was no discussion.

And apparently, he was rich. It had never occurred to Jennie that he could be. He owned this big house and farm, but that was something that had been handed down to him from his family. It didn't necessarily make him rich. From what she had heard, estates like this one required a lot of money to keep maintained and running, so it didn't automatically give a lot in return moneywise.

But this wasn't the only place he owned. He owned a huge estate back in America, much bigger than this one, and a large vineyard in the south of France. And as if that wasn't enough, he owned several successful businesses. So, the guy was loaded.

Jennie would have mated him regardless, and she had. She had known nothing of his wealth when she said yes to mating him; all she cared about was him. And she still did. No money could buy her this kind of happiness, and that was something she was going to teach her children if she ever had any.

She gasped. Protection. They had used no protection since they mated. It hadn't even occurred to her. She had been way too horny and focused on Trevor.

Trevor stopped and turned to her. "What is it?" He was staring at her with a worried expression on his face.

"Condoms. We forgot to use them. I might be..." She trailed off, not sure how he would react.

He seemed stunned for a second, and Jennie prepared herself to talk him down. The chance of her getting pregnant so fast was small, and they would be careful in the future.

She wasn't prepared for the happy grin that spread across his face.

"Would that be so bad?" Trevor's eyes were shining

with joy and pride. "It might be a bit soon, but I can't wait to see your belly grow with my pup. You'd be even more stunning than you are now, even though I'm not sure if that's possible."

Jennie threw her arms around his neck and hugged him firmly. "I love you. You're the most amazing man I've ever met." Then, she loosened her hold on him and pulled back enough to look into his eyes. "And I'd love to have your children, but I wouldn't mind waiting a little while, until I've gotten to know you better. I want to have time to enjoy being the two of us before bringing a third person into our midst."

Trevor smiled down at her. "Whatever you want. I guess we'll try to remember those condoms from now on then."

***

Looking into Jennie's eyes, Trevor couldn't believe his luck. He had never expected mating to be this amazing. Sure, he had seen a lot of mated couples and how happy they were just being together, but he had also seen the alpha females and how they tended to drive their men a little crazy. But maybe he hadn't been paying attention to the underlying love between the couples, and how that craziness was some of the spice that kept the fire going in their relationship.

He had always hated the fact that he was expected to mate an alpha female, but suddenly he understood why. That was what he needed. Someone to stand up to him who wouldn't just allow him to take charge and run the show. It turned him on and gave their relationship another dimension.

Jennie liked that he took charge in bed, and she liked the way he took care of her, but he would never be able to boss her around. And he liked that about her. She was fierce and had no problem standing up for herself, or him, when necessary. She might not be a wolf, but she was an alpha female. His alpha female.

ⲟⲟⲟⲟⲟ

Michael was staring out of the train window, but he didn't really notice the scenery flying by outside.

So much had changed in the last few days, and him sitting there alone on the way back to Edinburgh was not part of his plan. He had thought Jennie would be his by the time they headed back from Fearolc, and that by securing her as his mate, he would have screwed up his father's plans for him. Instead, Michael had wasted a week on a woman who didn't want him, and he couldn't even blame her. He had acted like an arrogant jerk toward her. Then again, he had never really stood a chance. Jennie was a wolf's true mate. There was no way around something like that. And deep down he was happy for her. She deserved the bliss he had seen in her eyes, and so did the wolf. Trevor was a decent man, and Michael respected him more than he had ever done his own father.

Michael had always thought that true mates were like the couples he knew from his clowder, his parents being one of those. The man was the one in charge, and the woman did what she was told without complaining. Otherwise, she would be punished and publicly humiliated.

But this week had shown him something else. He had thought James and Carlos weren't men enough to handle their women, but that wasn't what he had observed on this trip. Ann and Marna loved their mates more than anything and would stand by their men no matter what happened. Not because they were scared of them or knew they would get punished if they didn't, but because they loved and respected their husbands. This dedication didn't in any way make the women weak, however. Both of them would stand up to their husbands and express their opinions if they felt that was necessary, but they would do it with respect and love. And for some reason, that made James and Carlos seem more manly and not less.

He could see the same relationship traits developing between Trevor and Jennie. Trevor was a strong alpha, actually one of the most powerful alphas Michael had ever met, yet Trevor had no qualms about openly showing his affection and love for Jennie. And the love and bond between the mates seemed to make Trevor even more powerful.

The train slowing down had Michael waking up from his contemplations. They were approaching the station in Fort William.

Stephanie. Thoughts of the woman had visited him regularly since he had carried her down from the mountain. How was she doing? Was she still in the hospital? Or had she already been discharged? He didn't even know her last name, so he didn't think he would be able to find her even if he tried. And why would he want to try anyway? He was clearly becoming desperate. It was probably the dread of what he knew would happen when he got back from this trip that was affecting him.

Michael was just turning away from the window when his eyes caught a familiar face outside. His heart rate sped up when he recognized Stephanie between two men, in a large parking lot close to the train station. The men seemed to be supporting her as she slowly limped between them. While he was watching, Stephanie stumbled, and the man on her right yanked her upright without breaking his stride. The pain on Stephanie's face didn't escape Michael. She was in no condition to be walking around on her fractured leg. What the fuck were those guys doing to her? And why didn't she scream for help? There were other people close by in the parking lot.

The train was slowing to a stop at the station, and suddenly there was a fence blocking Michael's view of Stephanie. Before he even realized what he was doing, he grabbed his jacket and his bag and made his way to the closest door. As soon as the train came to a full stop and the doors opened, he exited and hurried into the station. He quickly found the exit closest to the parking lot and ran out the door and around the corner.

Michael entered at the corner of the large parking area. He scanned the lot quickly and recognized one of the cruel men who had walked with Stephanie. The man opened the door of a large gray van and swung himself into the passenger seat. The van started speeding away before Michael could get close enough to see if Stephanie was in the vehicle, but it wasn't a stretch to assume she had been put into the storage area in the back of the van.

There was no way he would be able to catch up with the moving vehicle, not in his human form, anyway. He followed the van with his eyes while it drove through a roundabout and pulled onto the main road going north. At least he had a direction and the license plate number. It wasn't a lot to go on, but it was more than nothing.

The train had already left by the time he came back into the station. He pulled his cell phone out of his pocket and sent a quick text to James to explain that he had something to take care of and would meet them in Edinburgh later. Then he made his way to the information desk.

A few minutes later, he was walking along the main street going north toward the only hospital in Fort William.

ooooo

Stephanie was lying on the dirty floor in the back of the van. She had been stupid to think she could hide in the hospital. The false name she had given them hadn't been enough to prevent Jack's goons from finding her. As soon as she had realized they were on their way to her room, she had gotten out of there. But she hadn't been able to get far. She wasn't exactly in the condition to run.

There would be no more escaping. Steph had managed to get away from Jack once, but look where that had gotten her. To the hospital with a broken leg. If only she had been a bit more careful up there in the hills, but her only focus had been to get as far away as possible. She hadn't been watching where she was going, and she had taken a fall because of it. Steph should have died up there; it would have been for the best, but instead she had met Him.

Michael. She had honestly thought she was in

heaven when she saw him. Features like an angel with light-brown eyes staring at her with concern. He immediately took charge and made sure she was as comfortable as she could be under the circumstances. Steph had felt so safe, and for a minute, she had actually dared to believe that everything would turn out well. That her nightmare was finally over.

The feel of his strong arms around her as he carried her down from the mountain would forever be a cherished memory. And if she hadn't been in so much pain at the time, the feel of his rock-hard abs against her side would have made her body heat up for him. Good thing it didn't because he might have been able to scent her arousal.

There was no doubt in her mind that Michael was a shifter. No regular man would have been able to carry her all the way down from the mountain like he did. And yet she wasn't scared of him like she was of the other shifters she knew. Michael wasn't like them. He was different.

Then she was in the ambulance, driving away from him. Steph had begged him to come with her, and for a second, the look in his eyes had given her hope. But then he had left her side, and they had closed the doors between them, forever shutting him out of her life.

If only she could find the courage to end her life. It would be better than what was awaiting her. Mate to the alpha panther, the most vicious and cruel man she had ever met.

---THE END---

BOOKS BY CAROLINE S. HILLIARD

Highland Shifters

A Wolf's Unlikely Mate, Book 1
Taken by the Cat, Book 2
Wolf Mate Surprise, Book 3
Seduced by the Monster, Book 4
Tempted by the Wolf, Book 5
Pursued by the Panther, Book 6
True to the Wolf, Book 7 – May 2023
Book 8 – TBA

Troll Guardians

Captured by the Troll, Book 1
Saving the Troll, Book 2
Book 3 – TBA

ABOUT THE AUTHOR

Thank you for reading my book. I hope the story gave you a nice little break from normality.

I have always loved reading and immersing myself in different worlds. Recently I have discovered that I also love writing. Stories have been playing in my head for as long as I can remember, and now I'm taking the time to develop some of these stories and write them down. Spending time in a world of my own creation has been a surprising enjoyment, and I hope to spend as much time as possible writing in the years to come.

I'm an independent author, meaning that I can write what I want and when I want. I primarily write for myself, but hopefully my stories can brighten someone else's day as well. The characters I develop tend to take on a life of their own and push the story in the direction they want, which means that the stories do not follow a set structure or specific literary style. However, I'm a huge fan of happily ever after, so that is a guarantee.

I'm married and the mother of two teenagers. Life is busy with a fulltime job in addition to family life. Writing is something I enjoy in my spare time.

You can find me here:
caroline.s.hilliard@gmail.com
www.carolineshilliard.com
www.facebook.com/Author.CarolineS.Hilliard/
www.amazon.com/author/carolineshilliard/
www.goodreads.com/author/show/22044909.Caroline_S_Hilliard

Printed in Great Britain
by Amazon

23175789R00165